Mirror, Mirror

SPINETINGLERS

#18

Mirror, Mirror

M. T. COFFIN

AN AVON CAMELOT BOOK

VISIT OUR WEBSITE AT
http://AvonBooks.com

MIRROR, MIRROR is an original publication of Avon Books. This work has never before appeared in book form.

AVON BOOKS
A division of
The Hearst Corporation
1350 Avenue of the Americas
New York, New York 10019

Copyright © 1997 by Kathleen Duey
Excerpt from *Boogey's Back for Blood* copyright © 1997 by Michael Vlessides
Published by arrangement with the author
Library of Congress Catalog Card Number: 96-96901
ISBN: 0-380-78611-7
RL: 4.9

First Avon Camelot Printing: February 1997

CAMELOT TRADEMARK REG. U.S. PAT. OFF. AND IN OTHER COUNTRIES, MARCA REGISTRADA, HECHO EN U.S.A.

Printed in the U.S.A.

OPM 10 9 8 7 6 5 4 3 2 1

Jake Dement sat still, staring down into his desk at school. Rob Phillips had been busy. To make things even worse, it was a hot day, the kind southern California can get any time of the year, if the winds come in from the desert. So even though it was December third, it was eighty-five degrees outside.

Jake felt like he was going to explode. He imagined it for a second. If he did blow up, he wanted most of the mess to land on Rob. Jake had left his desk to go to the bathroom. Somehow, in that four-minute span, Rob had managed to play another trick on him. This time it was a particularly clever hot-day kind of trick. Rob had put a big glob of dessert gelatin in his desk.

Jake glared at the green, shivery little mound beside his schoolbooks. It was starting to melt. Rob was a genius at rotten tricks. Soon it would puddle out far enough to get on his books and his lunch

1

sack. Jake closed his desk quietly and looked at the clock. About five minutes until lunch recess. Then he'd go get paper towels and wipe up the green goo.

He got so angry at Rob's tricks that it scared him sometimes. He wanted to turn and stare at Rob so hard that Rob would just shrink and wither away like the wicked witch in *The Wizard of Oz*. He could imagine it perfectly, every detail vivid and complete. He had envisioned it a dozen times when he was angry at Rob and there was nothing else he *could* do. The puddle would be black and sticky.

Jake shifted in his desk and looked at the clock. Four minutes to recess. Mrs. Richards was winding up their history lesson, still talking about the Civil War. He tried to listen, but it was hard. In fact, the situation at school was getting worse. Rob pulled some kind of trick on him nearly every day. At first it had just been stupid notes, or hiding Jake's homework in the wrong book. Lately Rob was getting more and more creative.

Yesterday there had been a mustard sandwich in his lunch sack—a huge dripping glob of yellow between two slices of gluey white bread—switched for his usual pastrami on rye. Rob had probably eaten Jake's sandwich while he was laughing about Jake being stuck with a lunch no one could eat. Rob had such a wonderful sense of humor. The day before that, Jake had opened his math book and a dozen dead caterpillars had fallen out, all over his desk and onto the floor. They had been smashed, staining the page. Their flattened little bodies had made Jake even angrier. It was just like Rob Phillips to think that killing something was funny.

Mrs. Richards was drawing a diagram on the board. She loved to draw, and she was good at it. All her lines were straight, and her printing was neat and easy to read. This diagram was of Civil War battle fortifications. She was explaining how the Confederate soldiers had dug trenches near the city of Vicksburg to guard it against the Yankee forces.

"Did they sleep in the trenches?" Don Blair asked. He lived across the street from Jake, but Jake barely knew him. It seemed like every day after school Don was either locked into his computer or out playing football with friends. Unless it was about history or football, Don Blair wasn't very interested.

As the history lesson continued, Jake tried to pay attention, but he felt a little drop of melting gelatin hit his pants. He slid his legs to one side. The green slime was seeping out of the metal bottom of his desk where the bolts connected it to the base. Too angry to control himself any longer, he gave in and glared across the room at Rob.

Rob was smiling at him, wearing an expression that said they were friends and he was just delighted to catch Jake looking at him. Jake fought to stay calm. It would be great if he really could make Rob wither and melt . . . like gelatin on a

3

hot, sunny day, just like this gooey stuff in his desk. He imagined it again, Rob's legs getting shorter, liquefying into a puddle.

Jake looked down and saw his face reflected in the shiny inner spine of his three-ring binder. He took a quick breath. The reflection was strange— his face was so distorted with anger that he didn't even look like himself. It was eerie. As Jake stared, the reflection winked at him, a slow, deliberate wink.

Jake looked up, his heart speeding. Reflections did not wink unless the person being reflected did, and he was sure he hadn't. He focused his eyes on the chalkboard, forcing himself to listen to Mrs. Richards.

". . . So people came from all over the world to fight in the Civil War. There were young European gentlemen, infatuated with one side's cause or the other and looking for adventure." Mrs. Richards glanced at the clock. "We'll talk more about the Civil War tomorrow. Get ready for lunch, please."

Jake had to open his desk again to get out his lunch bag. The gelatin had melted a little more. He shoved his books back, farther away from it. Rob had started playing tricks like this during the second week of school. Now it was almost Christmas, and he was still trying to get even. It was all because of a stupid basketball game.

Back in September, during Jake's first week of school at Finlay Elementary, it had rained for three days straight. When it finally stopped, everyone poured outside for recess, shouting and excited. Looking back, Jake wished he had lost that day, playing one-on-one basketball with Rob. But he hadn't known Rob then, and his father had taught him to always play hard and fair. Rob played hard, too, but he also cheated.

About the tenth time Rob stuck his elbow into Jake's ribs that day in September, Jake had gotten angry. He had started to play even harder, and he had started to win.

A few boys had stopped to watch them, then a few more. They were both pretty good, and the competition was almost even. Twice, Rob had gotten four points ahead, but then Jake had caught up and taken the lead. Finally, Rob had begun to get tired.

By then, half the fifth grade was watching. Rob made a clumsy play and stumbled backward, off the edge of the asphalt. He lost his balance, sitting down hard in a mud puddle left by the rain. When he stood up, it looked like his backside had been dipped in chocolate. Everyone laughed. Rob stomped off, went to the nurse, and waited for his mother to bring him clean pants.

Two girls who had the flu and were waiting for their parents to come overheard the whole thing and spread the news all over school. Rob's mother was upset because it was hard for her to leave work, so Rob got a lecture from her about playing in the mud like a baby. Everyone repeated the rumor, and Jake knew both girls—they weren't big gossips. So it was true. The whole school laughed about it for a week or two.

On the day it happened, Jake hadn't understood why everyone thought it was so funny for Rob to fall down and get muddy. He knew now. Rob had been picking on other kids for so long that everyone was glad when something finally happened to him. Almost no one liked Rob, and the few kids who acted like they did were probably just afraid of him. Rob was a bully. He was always picking on someone. He was big, and he seemed to love making other kids afraid of him.

The lunch bell rang. Jake stood up. Instead of going to the cafeteria, he'd go get paper towels from the bathroom and come back. That way he could clean up the mess while no one was looking. As he waited for the room to clear out, he thought about telling Mrs. Richards what Rob had done, but he'd already tried that and it hadn't worked. Mrs. Richards would talk to Rob, of course, but it would only make matters worse. Jake shook his head, remembering his face reflected in his binder spine. He had enough problems with Rob. The last thing he needed was to start imagining things.

The first time Jake had gone to Mrs. Richards, Rob had waited for him after school to threaten him. Then the tricks had gotten worse. The second time, Rob had promised to make his life miserable, and he had. It was awful, waiting every day to see what was going to happen next. And it was impossible to make friends. No one wanted to take the risk of becoming Rob's next target.

Rob was doing exactly what he'd threatened to do. This was the most miserable school year of Jake's whole life. He'd stopped trying to get help from Mrs. Richards. He hadn't even said much to his mother about it. What good could it possibly do?

During recess, Don Blair hung around for a few minutes, talking to Mrs. Richards. Don lived across the street from Jake—they'd met the day Jake's family had moved in, four months ago. But all Don ever wanted to do was to watch, play, or talk about football. Jake hated football, so they weren't really friends yet. Maybe after the Super Bowl was over, they could find something to do together. Jake smiled at Don and he smiled back, but didn't say anything as he went out for recess.

Once Don left and Mrs. Richards had gone to the teachers' lounge, Jake hustled down the hall and into the bathroom. He brought a huge wad of paper towels and managed to get the blob of green goo out of his desk and into the trash without anyone noticing.

Then he sat on the edge of his desk and just stared out the window at the playground. Rob was out there somewhere, waiting for him to come out so he could hassle him. You had to give him points for effort—and creativity. Gelatin was the perfect mess-making substance to use. It was solid enough to handle easily, then it would melt. How had Rob kept it from melting before he'd put it inside the desk? Had he brought a cooler to school and hidden it somewhere? It seemed like he was willing to go to any amount of trouble to make sure his mean stunts worked out right. Jake wondered when Rob would decide they were even. Would he ever?

After school, Jake walked home. As usual, Rob stepped on the backs of his shoes for the first three blocks, then kept going straight when Jake turned down his street. Jake sighed. One more day of Rob's tricks was finished, but now he had to go home—and that meant he had to deal with Becca and Tracy.

"Jaaaaaakkkkkkke!"

Jake heard his sisters' voices as he came down the sidewalk. He felt his stomach tighten. He could have used some time alone. As he watched his five-year-old twin sisters racing across the lawn to meet him, he knew he wasn't going to get it. Maybe, he thought, if he ran fast and didn't stop, he could beat the twins to the top of the stairs, get into his room, and lock the door. He hitched his backpack higher and was about to break into a run when his mother appeared on the front steps.

"I am so glad you're home," she called. "The new manager phoned. They need me to come in to work tonight."

Jake slumped back into a slow walk. Terrific.

8

That meant he'd end up babysitting his sisters for at least two hours until his father came home. What a perfect day. What a completely wonderful, perfect day it had been. It could hardly get better unless the earth opened up and swallowed him. He shook his head, smiling wryly at his own gloomy thoughts. It was amazing how Rob was changing his outlook on life. Jake loved his sisters; it was just that they got on his nerves sometimes. His mother kept saying that when they got a little older, they'd be less work and more fun. But it seemed she'd been saying that since they were babies.

"Hi, Jake!" Becca yelled.

"Hi, Jake!" Tracy echoed. They ran in a tight circle around him as he crossed the lawn. It made him dizzy to watch them. They almost never stopped moving.

"Guess what?" Becca shouted. It was her new favorite saying. There probably wasn't anything to guess. Most likely, nothing interesting had happened. She just loved to make people ask, "What?"

"Guess what?" Tracy chimed in. "Guess what? Guess what?"

The twins started to sing the words, still chasing each other around Jake as he walked. He refused to respond. Becca gave up when they were almost at the porch steps, but Tracy chanted "Guess what?" all the way upstairs.

"*What?*" Jake shouted at them, as he went into

his room. They were right on his heels, of course. They always were, unless they were sick or had gone somewhere with his parents. They fell into a giggle-heap on his bed, rolling and squealing.

"They just worship the ground you walk on," Jake's mother said from the doorway.

He nodded wearily and slid out of his backpack.

His mother smiled apologetically. "I'm sorry about tonight. I told them I don't want any more of these dinner shifts. But . . ."

"The new manager needs you, and we need the money," Jake finished for her. "I know, Mom. It's only a few hours. It'll be all right."

"You're terrific," his mother said, and she looked so relieved that he had to smile at her. She whirled and went out, calling back over her shoulder, "I have to get going. Frances has the flu and had to leave early. That means they're shorthanded now."

Jake nodded and waved at her, even though she was already halfway down the hall.

"What do you want to play?" Tracy demanded.

"Let's play Sharks," Becca said firmly.

Jake sighed. "Sharks" was a game he had invented to keep the twins in one place. They pretended that his bed was a fishing boat, and that they were surrounded by shark-infested waters. Every time one of them tried to jump off the bed, he would yell, "Shark!" and they would race back, giggling hysterically.

10

"Don't get off," Becca said, starting the game. "I see sharks."

"So do I," Tracy agreed.

Jake got on the bed, stretching out next to the wall. He rolled over and faced away from the twins, staring at little chipped places in the white paint. He just wanted to be alone for a while—was that so much to ask? He felt himself getting angry again, a hot, uncomfortable feeling, like he was going to explode.

He rolled back over and sat up. The late-afternoon sun coming in his window reflected off the glass that covered his favorite photograph, a picture of a watering hole on the African plains, dotted with wildebeests and zebras. *That* was where he wanted to be. He wanted to be anyplace where there were no jerks like Rob Phillips and no twin sisters to shriek and squeal when what he needed was peace and quiet. He would come back someday, when the twins were sixteen and he was twenty-two and Rob Phillips had moved to some other state . . . *any* other state.

"Sharks!" Becca yelled, extending one hand, then snatching it back as though a great white had leapt from the carpet to chomp it off. She screamed— or pretended to, anyway—and they both collapsed, giggling madly again. Their voices were so high pitched, the sound hurt Jake's ears. He tried to smile at his sisters. In a few minutes, he would make them leave. They could go play in their own room for a while. He felt the phony smile droop and let it. He didn't really feel much like smiling.

Jake stared at the rectangle of sunlight glinting off the glass in the picture frame. There was an elongated slanting reflection of his room. He could see himself in the frame, he realized, scowling and angry looking.

For a moment he just studied himself, trying to see details in the vague, ghostlike reflection. Then, as the twins screamed another shark alarm, a cold shock went through Jake's body. The reflection didn't show him lying on his bed; it showed him standing up, his arms crossed, by his dresser on the opposite wall. Or was it him? Jake glanced across the room, but of course there was no one else standing there. How could there be?

He looked back at the picture. The image was gone. Now he was reflected exactly as he had been all along, lying down, frowning, getting a headache from his sisters' noise.

"I'm taking off now," Jake's mother called down the hallway.

"Okay," he yelled back, feeling strange. He rubbed his hands across his face. The twins were bouncing and shrieking, having a wonderful time dodging imaginary sharks. They acted as if they were really terrified, but Jake knew that if he asked them if the sharks were real, they'd laugh at him and think he was being silly.

Jake exhaled a long breath. If his little sisters

knew the difference between make-believe and reality, what was wrong with him? He had to go to bed early tonight. Rob Phillips and the twins' noise were driving him past his breaking point. He really was imagining things.

2

Jake woke up Saturday morning to a silent house. It was so quiet that he got up, instead of lying in bed as he usually did on weekends. He wandered down the hall and past the bathroom to the twins' door. He pressed his ear against the smooth white wood, puzzled.

"Becca? Tracy?" He heard only silence in response. He pushed the door open slowly, silently. Maybe they were both still asleep? But their beds were empty, and neatly made—which meant his mother had done it.

Jake padded back up the hall and went down the stairs. In the kitchen there was a note that explained everything.

Dear Jake,

We took the girls to the zoo. We'll be gone at least until noon, or maybe later, if they don't

14

get too cranky and tired. Enjoy your morning. We were going to wake you and take you with us, but your father says you'd probably prefer a little time to yourself. You certainly earned it babysitting last night! Thanks again. See you soon.

Mom and Dad

Jake stared at the note for a minute, almost unable to believe it. A whole morning, alone? Then he looked at the clock and flinched. It was already almost ten o'clock. He had slept in and wasted half his precious morning—he knew that no matter what his mother said, the twins wouldn't last at the zoo for more than a few hours.

Jake's father loved animals, and he had taken them all to the zoo a zillion times. The twins had been there so often that they knew their way around, and it was a big place. They would want to see their favorite elephant and feed their favorite goat at the petting zoo, and then check on the hippo to see if she'd had her baby yet. But after that, if they were grumpy at all, they would start to argue.

Jake looked around the kitchen. He wasn't sure whether he should have a big breakfast and sit down and eat it slowly and enjoy it in the quiet, or fix something quick and small so that he could just eat and then . . . Jake rubbed his hand through his hair. And then *what?*

He could walk across the street and see if Don Blair wanted to ride bikes or play basketball or something, but he knew that Don wouldn't want to do either. Don would be down at the vacant lot, getting into the usual Saturday morning flag football game. Jake considered going, then he looked out the window.

The weather had changed, the sky was gray; the desert winds had reversed. This morning looked foggy, maybe even cloudy. Sometimes, this time of year, the fog really got thick. It might be gray all day—no sunshine at all.

Jake stood up. He would waste the whole two hours if he wasn't careful. He turned in a circle and faced the cupboards. Cereal. Small and quick. He reached up and opened the cupboard above the dishwasher. But just as he took out the granola, the phone rang.

Jake set the box down on the counter and whirled around to run for the phone. He felt his sleeve snag the box and heard the crash, but he didn't look back as he crossed the kitchen. As he picked up the phone, he heard a roll of thunder outside. It wasn't just fog; a storm had rolled in. He said hello.

"Jake?"

It was his mother. "Oh," he said. "Hi."

"It's starting to drizzle here, Jake," she said. "I'm sorry, but we're probably going to have to start home. Your father said I should call you and let you know."

16

He stood very still. Of course. *Of course* today would be the first rainy day after weeks of warm weather. *Of course* his parents and the twins were going to come home early. Why not? If they'd stayed, he actually might have had a fun morning.

"Jake?"

"Yeah."

"Did you hear me?"

Jake nodded. "How could I not hear you? The phone is on my ear."

"I'm really sorry, Jake."

Jake tried not to sound like a jerk. "Sure, Mom. It's okay. Goodbye."

He hung up, feeling lousy. It wasn't his mother's fault, and he knew that. But he had really wanted to have the morning to himself—just one morning of peace and quiet. He turned and looked back across the kitchen. He almost felt like crying. There was granola all over the floor. The little crunchy pieces had skidded all the way across to the kitchen table.

He fought an urge to throw his cereal bowl across the room, too. Before he could get all this cleaned up, they'd be back. The twins would leap around and scatter the granola even farther. They'd track it into the living room and up into their bedroom before anyone could stop them or even slow them down.

Outside the thunder rolled again. Well, at least it was perfect weather for the mood he was in. He

17

heard a few drops of rain spatter against the roof. Just then the doorbell rang. He sat still for a few seconds, wishing whoever it was would just go away.

Jake's parents had strict rules about opening the door. If he was home alone, he had to peek through the dining room window and see who it was. If it was someone he knew, or a kid from school he recognized, he could answer. If it was a stranger or an adult, any adult except Aunt Sandy or one of his parents, he was to pretend not to be home. If the adult was doing something suspicious—like if they hung around instead of leaving after no one answered—Jake was supposed to call Mr. Johnson, a neighbor who was a retired policeman.

Jake went quickly into the dining room and knelt to part the curtains a half inch. He couldn't see anyone at first. Then he focused through the bushes in the planter and saw Rob Phillips crouching on the porch. Jake watched carefully. Rob lived only two streets over, but Jake almost never saw him except when they were in school or walking home. He hadn't thought Rob even knew which house was his.

Jake gripped the edge of the curtain and fought an urge to scream aloud. His Saturday morning—his perfect, quiet Saturday morning—had now been ruined twice. Not only would he get no time off from his sisters; he had to deal with Rob on a Saturday, during the tiny little bit of privacy and quiet he had ended up with.

Jake backed away from the curtains. If he opened the door suddenly, it would startle Rob and he'd have to stammer out some reason why he was there. That would be interesting, at least. Rob would have to make something up, and it might even scare him away if Jake pretended his father was home. Maybe he'd fling open the door and tell Rob his father wanted to know what Rob was doing on their porch. Half smiling, Jake started toward the front hall, then hesitated. What was Rob up to? If he was playing a trick . . .

Jake stopped in his tracks. Maybe he should call Mr. Johnson.

It had never done any good to talk to Mrs. Richards about Rob's pranks. When she lectured Rob, it only made him more determined. And his parents would only advise him to ignore Rob, or to try to understand why he was a bully. But what if Mr. Johnson were to come leaping out of the bushes? He was big and bald and kind of scary looking. He had a rough, scratchy voice, and he wouldn't think vandalism was funny at all. He hated kids who got into trouble—in fact, Jake wasn't sure he liked kids of any kind. Maybe Mr. Johnson could scare Rob into leaving him alone.

Jake went back to the dining room and peeked out again. Rob was nowhere to be seen. Had he left? Jake ran from one window to the next, peering

19

out carefully, glad his mother hadn't opened the curtains that morning.

Rob wasn't anywhere in the front yard. Jake stood up straight and exhaled, half in relief and half in disappointment. Then he had a thought. He ran up the stairs. From his bedroom window, Jake could see the whole backyard. But Rob wasn't there, either. He had either decided to go home, or . . . he had already played whatever trick he had come for.

Jake ran back downstairs. He veered into the dining room for another quick look. Rob was no longer on the porch steps. He wasn't on the front lawn or on the sidewalk. Thunder rumbled, and Jake heard a second spate of raindrops on the roof. He went to the front door and flung it open. There, on the top step, was a dog poop, arranged perfectly, just as though some dog had climbed the steps to make a mess on their porch.

Jake looked around for a stick. He finally found one and pushed Rob's present into the planter, then hosed down the concrete. He felt silly, using the hose in the middle of a rainstorm. It was really starting to come down hard now.

Once the concrete was clean again, Jake went back inside, fuming as he slammed the door shut. Was Rob going to start coming to the house? What was wrong with him? Didn't he have anything else to do with his weekends? Didn't he have anything better to do with his *life?*

Jake banged his way back into the kitchen. He should have called Mr. Johnson the instant he'd seen Rob. He shouldn't have wasted a second. If Rob ever dared to come back, that was exactly what he was going to do. He'd tell Mr. Johnson about this trick, and the gelatin, and . . . Jake shook his head. He was going to feel stupid telling Mr. Johnson about Rob. Mr. Johnson was tough and strong. If anyone had ever played these kinds of tricks on him, he would have found a way to make them stop, not gone running to teachers and parents and neighbors for help. Mr. Johnson would probably tell Jake to stand up for himself. And maybe that was what he should do. But the truth was, he was afraid of Rob.

Angry at himself, Jake found the broom and dustpan and started cleaning up the cereal mess. As he worked, he kept feeling fresh waves of fury go through him. Rob Phillips was going to be sorry. Someday, somehow, Jake was going to get even with him. He was going to figure out a way to make Rob leave him alone if it took the whole rest of the school year and next summer, too.

When the cereal had been swept up off the floor, Jake poured a glass of juice, got a carton of fruit yogurt from the fridge and a spoon, and sat down at the kitchen table. He sat still, knowing he would hear his parents and his sisters at the front door any second now. He opened the yogurt, then just

21

stared at it, rocking his spoon back and forth on the table.

He could just imagine what the rest of the day was going to be like. The twins would be noisy when they got home, full of stories about the zoo. Then they'd start to get bored and antsy from being cooped up in the house. He could hear rain cascading over the roof. They would want him to play with them and they'd get upset if he didn't. If he went into his room, they would pound up and down the hall outside his door, shrieking and playing— or arguing. Eventually, they would knock on his door, even if their mother told them not to. It wasn't fair that he'd have to spend his day locked up in his room.

Jake held up his spoon and rolled it between his fingers, staring past it at the light fixture in the center of the ceiling. Then his eyes happened to fall on the shiny convex surface of the spoon itself.

For an instant, Jake saw his own face, dark with anger. Then he saw something that made his heart thump so hard that it hurt. The same distorted face that he'd seen in his binder was suddenly staring back at him. It winked again—another slow, deliberate wink, as though they shared a secret.

Jake felt weird and dizzy. He set the spoon down and refused to look at it. This could not be happening. How could a spoon reflect a face that wasn't his?

Jake looked up at the ceiling, toward the door, out the window, then back at the spoon. The face was still there. He stared at it, his heart beating so hard it almost hurt. It was a strange face. It looked a lot like his own face, with sandy hair and freckles—but not quite. The reflection's nose was too small, the mouth was a little too crooked, and the eyes were wide and intense. Jake swallowed, his throat dry. Something was wrong with the face. It didn't look exactly . . . human. Jake felt cold prickles of fear on the back of his neck.

"Jake?"

He heard the sound of a key in the lock. "We're back," his mother called out, as she pushed the door open. She sounded frazzled. He could hear the twins arguing about something. Their voices were high and squeaky when they were upset.

He saw his father pass the kitchen door, headed for the den. He waved. "Hi, Jake."

"Hi, Dad," Jake said quickly. What would his father think if he told him what he'd just seen? His father hated anything that didn't make sense. He would probably decide that something was very wrong with his son. Jake swallowed and pulled in a deep breath. Maybe there was.

Jake stood up and carried his dishes to the sink. As he set the spoon in, he risked a quick look at it. There was nothing there. He lifted it closer to his eye. All he saw were the ceiling lights, and then, as he turned it, his own face. So he was imagining everything?

"Of course I am," Jake muttered to himself, as his sisters ran into the kitchen, racing each other to the refrigerator. "How could it be real?" It couldn't, of course. But he didn't know whether he should feel good or bad about the realization.

Becca made it to the fridge first. "Chocolate milk!" she piped. She turned, jumping up and down in a circle.

Tracy pushed at her. "Mom said I could—not you."

Becca stumbled backward, bumping into the stove. She erupted into tears, her sobs high and shrill.

24

"Come on, you two," Jake pleaded. He saw his mother in the doorway.

"I'm sorry," she said immediately. "We wanted to give you a little time alone. But it's really pouring now."

Jake nodded. "I know. Thanks for trying." He said it loudly enough so that she could hear him over the twins. His mother smiled at him, then waded into the argument.

Jake watched her pull the twins apart, insisting that they had to be nice to each other and that there was plenty of chocolate milk for both of them. He wondered if she ever got as tired of the twins' noise as he did. Probably.

Jake took a deep breath, thinking. Maybe that was what was making him see things that weren't really there. He had heard about it on TV. Stress could make a person experience all kinds of weird things. Some people actually got chest pains, as if they were having a heart attack, when they weren't at all. Jake shook his head. Having chest pains wasn't the same thing as imagining faces that couldn't possibly be there—was it?

"I want to play Tents," Becca was yelling. They both seemed to have forgotten completely about chocolate milk. Tracy was singing a song she had learned at their day-care center. Both twins loved to sing—loudly. The song changed now as Tracy joined in. It had started out being about a boy and his dog. Now it was about a boy and his tent.

Jake saw his mother straighten up, holding her hands out as the twins leapt in circles. "Okay, okay, *okay.*" She walked to the hall linen closet and pulled out the old sheets she kept for rainy-day tents. The twins ran with them, scuttling up the stairs. Jake's mother turned to face him. "They said they were hungry all the way home. Now they've forgotten entirely."

"They'll remember once they get their tents made."

Jake watched his mother laugh. She looked tired. "No doubt. Well . . . how was your morning? I know it was too short, but otherwise, how was it?"

He smiled. "Too short. And a kid from school came by." Jake hesitated, unsure whether he should tell his mother about Rob.

It was too late; her eyes had focused on him. "Who?"

Jake wished he hadn't said anything. His mother had an amazing ability to pick up on stuff that was bothering him. He was careful not to mention Rob Phillips very often. She knew Rob harassed him at school once in a while, but she had no idea how much trouble Rob really caused. If she had known, she'd have gone to the principal a long time ago. That would make Rob so angry that he would never give up, Jake was sure.

And Rob is sure giving up the way things are, Jake chided himself silently and sarcastically. *Old Rob Phillips is just the nicest guy in the whole class now. It sure pays to ignore a bully. All you have to do is stick with it long enough. Right.*

"Jake?" His mother was looking at him intently.

"It was Rob Phillips," Jake said, deciding that maybe his mother should know, just in case she ever saw Rob poking around their house. "He dropped by to put a dog poop on the front porch."

"Say that again?" Jake's mother asked, a look of astonishment crossing her face.

Jake nodded. "You heard me. He came to put dog poop on the porch. He's the same one who plays tricks on me sometimes at school."

"Well, if he drops by again, I'll have a talk with him."

"Mom, please don't," Jake said quickly. "It doesn't help. He just gets worse."

"I've never talked to him before," his mother insisted. "How do you know how he'd react? Or maybe your dad should do it."

Jake shrugged. She was only echoing the thoughts he'd had a few seconds before. Ignoring Rob wasn't working. Maybe it *was* time to try something else. But Jake didn't want either of his parents talking to Rob Phillips. He was pretty sure it wouldn't help—after all, it hadn't helped when Mrs. Richards had talked to him—and it could make things a lot worse.

"Does he live around here?"

Jake nodded. "A couple of streets over."

"I think we should do something," his mother

27

said, distracted by the twins launching into a new game that involved chasing each other around the kitchen.

Jake turned to fiddle with his dishes in the sink, then looked at his mother again. He hadn't meant to start talking about Rob Phillips, and he certainly wasn't going to tell his mother that he'd seen a strange face in his cereal spoon. He cleared his throat. "It's nothing, Mom—really. Lots of kids play tricks."

His mother shook her head. "Someone who can't think of anything better to do with his Saturday morning than vandalize a neighbor's house needs a talking to. Have you spoken to Mrs. Richards?"

Jake nodded. "And it didn't help. If anything, he got mad about it and things got worse for a while."

Jake's mother was studying his face. "For a while? Is this the same boy you told me about a few months ago?" Jake nodded slowly. His mother looked upset. "And it hasn't gotten any better?"

Jake shrugged. "In a way it has. He stopped picking on me every recess." *Because I stay out of his way,* Jake thought to himself. *Because I either think of ways to stay in the classroom or run every time I see him coming.* "I think I'll go up and try to read a little bit, okay?" Jake said. He waited until his mother nodded, then he headed for the stairs. The twins followed.

In his room, with the door securely shut, it was almost peaceful. Jake could hear his sisters shrieking and laughing, back in their room down the hall. But it wasn't too loud. At least they weren't running up and down the hallway or leaning on his door, giggling and calling him. He could pretty much ignore it if he tried. So he tried.

He got down some of his favorite books, mostly science fiction. Then he turned on his little reading light and pulled down the shades so he wouldn't have to look at the rain outside. He got himself all settled on his bed, with his pillow mashed up the way he liked it behind his head and his feet crossed. Then he tried to read. But he couldn't.

It wasn't the twins down the hall, or the ticking of the rain on his windows. It wasn't that he was still upset about Rob Phillips. He couldn't read because he couldn't concentrate on the book. Every ten or fifteen seconds, he kept looking up at the reflection on the glass over his photo of Africa. He didn't see anything but a smooth rectangle of dim light from his shaded window. But he couldn't stop looking. Was the guy reflected in the picture frame the same one he had seen looking back at him from his spoon in the kitchen?

Jake shook his head and tossed his book across the room. There wasn't a "guy." There was only his imagination, and it was getting the better of him. He got up and went down the hall. The twins had shut their door, and he was glad. If they saw him, they might decide they needed him to play with them. He went into the bathroom and flicked on

29

the light. For a second his heart stopped beating, then it began again with slow, heavy thuds.

For just an instant, not quite long enough for Jake to be sure he had seen it, the mirror had shown his own reflection, *and a second face,* as though someone were standing behind him, looking over his shoulder. Jake stared at the mirror. He saw himself looking back, his skin pale and his eyes round and startled looking. The face from his cereal spoon had disappeared. Or had it ever really been there? Jake felt creepy prickles of fear on his neck and scalp. His knees felt watery, and he couldn't look away from the mirror for a long time. If the mirror had held anything but his own reflection, it was gone now.

The rain ended Sunday night. Monday morning was cool and damp, but the sky was clear and the sun was incredibly bright. Everything looked shiny, like someone had dusted the whole world. Walking to school, Jake tried to enjoy the pretty morning, but he couldn't. He hadn't seen the strange face again, but he was scared that he would. The dread he felt was almost like carrying a weight on his back. It never left, never let him completely relax. He had started to tell his mother two or three times. But what could he say?

He kept his eyes on the ground. The sidewalks around him were filling up as he got closer to school. More and more kids were walking close to him, and he didn't feel like talking. He felt a rush of anger at Rob, and his sisters, and the man in the mirror. Here it was, a perfectly beautiful morning, and he couldn't enjoy it at all.

"Good morning," Rob Phillips said pleasantly from right behind him.

Caught off guard, Jake half turned as Rob stepped on the back of his shoe. He stumbled and almost lost his balance, but at least his shoe stayed on his heel. Rob stopped and looked at him, phony astonishment on his face. "Jake, are you all right?" he asked. "Did you trip over your own foot? Or was there a pebble on the sidewalk?"

The five or six kids close enough to see what was going on giggled or turned away so they wouldn't have to. Rob sometimes got angry at onlookers if they seemed to disapprove of him. No one ever dared to go get a teacher to help. They knew they'd be a target if they did.

Rob was smiling his nasty smile, and Jake glared at him. He was getting so sick of being hassled that getting beat up was starting to sound almost good. Maybe if he just got into a fight with Rob, Rob would consider the score settled once and for all. "Leave me alone," he said, as loudly as he could.

Rob's look of astonishment got so exaggerated that he almost looked like a cartoon character. His eyebrows were arched like bird's wings.

Just then the warning bell rang and everyone hurried a little faster down the sidewalk. Rob pulled at Jake's arm and made another phony cartoonish face—this time he looked concerned. "Do be careful, Jake. Look where you're going. I know you can't walk very well, but try to make it to class without falling down."

Something inside Jake snapped. Without allowing himself to think about what he was doing, Jake wrinkled up his nose, staring at Rob. "There's a weird smell," he said loudly. He saw several kids lift their heads to listen. "There's a weird smell," he repeated a little more loudly, just to make sure that everyone would hear. "It's dog poop. You smell like dog poop, Rob." He wrinkled his nose once more and made a whooshing sound with his breath. "Have you been playing with dog poop again, Rob?"

So many people laughed that Jake was startled. He heard kids repeating what he had said to others who'd been able to hear only part of it. Rob was turning bright pink; for a moment Jake thought he was going to explode and come at him. But Rob just clenched and unclenched his hands a few times, then turned and walked faster, disappearing around the corner of the building.

While everyone else hurried to make it to class on time, Jake walked a little slower, amazed at what he'd done. In a way, it had felt wonderful to come back at Rob. But in the long run it had probably been a mistake. The truth was, Rob held a grudge longer than anyone he had known—longer than anyone he'd ever even heard about.

Jake scuffed his feet. After months of carefully ignoring Rob, he had blown everything with one stupid joke. He'd embarrassed Rob in front of half

the school. Now the tricks would never end. *Never.*
Jake shuddered, imagining it. He probably would
get beat up now. Rob would wait for him one day
after school or come to the house again. And even
if that didn't happen, there'd be some prank every
day, one more mean trick that only Rob would take
the time to figure out and pull off.

As Jake went up the steps and through the heavy
double doors, the second bell rang. That meant he
had three minutes to get to class. Jake walked
faster, getting angrier and angrier with himself—
and with Rob.

Jake plopped into his seat just as the bell rang.
He felt Rob glaring at him, but he refused to look
at him. Jake opened his desk and slung his books
inside. He closed the lid slowly. He would have to
be on extra alert now, that much was sure. Rob
would try to get even for the dog poop insult—
maybe he'd try to ruin Jake's homework today.
Jake nodded to himself. He had better stay inside
for recess. He'd have to think of a reason. Maybe
he could pretend he hadn't done some of his homework. Mrs. Richards let people stay in from recess
if they had work to finish.

Jake settled into his seat, deciding. Okay. That
was what he would do. He'd have to fib to stay in
and guard his desk and waste his recess sitting
inside. It would work. But it made him even angrier. He'd have to give up a recess and do an assignment he'd already done, just to keep Rob away

from his desk. Jake risked a glance to his right, toward the back of the room. Rob was looking at him, of course. He didn't put on his phony smile this time, or any other fake expression. He looked like he hated Jake; his eyes were flinty and narrow, his mouth set in a thin line.

"This morning we are going to go to the library," Mrs. Richards said in her sunny "Monday mornings can be fun" voice. "It's book report time again."

Kids began to shuffle their feet. Desk lids creaked open and slammed down as kids put away their books or pulled out their backpacks. Jake bit his lip. Normally, he liked going to the library. He liked Mrs. Barners, the librarian. She was one of the smartest people on the face of the earth. She knew things that no one had any reason to know. But this morning, he had to worry even more than usual about Rob Phillips.

As the rest of the class stood up, preparing to file out the door, Jake was trying to guess what Rob would do. He would probably wait until they were in the library, then tell Mrs. Barners that he had to use the bathroom. That was the only excuse acceptable to Mrs. Barners for leaving her library, even for a minute.

Once he was out of the library, Rob could rush back to the classroom and get into Jake's desk to destroy his homework, or something. He wouldn't have time for an elaborate plan today, unless he had already made something up and the dog poop insult would just make him want to play whatever trick he already had planned. Jake caught his breath. Maybe Rob had brought more dog poop. It was not beyond possibility, Jake thought. Rob's tricks sometimes ran in cycles.

Before the gelatin, he'd had one week of lunch switching. Before that, Rob had waited each day after school to follow Jake home, stepping on the backs of his shoes every chance he got.

Jake got his backpack ready as the classroom got noisier. Rob was capable of just about anything as long as he was pretty sure he wouldn't get caught. And if he could somehow get out of the library, he probably wouldn't be. Or maybe he would try to lag behind now.

Jake pretended to have to tie his shoe, falling out of line just inside the door. He stood aside until he was sure that Rob had gone out into the hall. Then Jake went out, bringing up the rear of the class. He glanced back through the doorway. Maybe it would be smarter just to carry his books with him.

"What's the matter, Jake?" Mrs. Richards said, bringing up the rear and pausing just outside the door. "Forget something?" He shook his head. "Then I'm going to lock up." She took out a key ring with a shiny disk on it—a coin or medallion or something. She slid her key into the lock and turned it. "I have a few valuables in my desk today," she explained, as they started down the hall.

Jake fell into step beside her, smiling. Now he could enjoy his library hour. Suddenly, his smile froze on his lips and he could feel the blood draining out of his face.

Mrs. Richards had set her shiny key ring on top of the books she was carrying back to the library. The big medallion was lying angled toward Jake. Like a cheap, distorted mirror, it reflected the ceiling, the lights, his face. But it wasn't his, was it? Even though the image was fuzzy, Jake was sure he recognized the odd face he had seen reflected in his spoon, the picture frame, and the bathroom mirror.

"Jake? Are you all right?" Mrs. Richards shifted the books in her arms and freed one hand to pick up the keys. Released from staring at the murky image in the medallion, Jake blinked and looked up. Mrs. Richards' eyes were full of concern. "Jake? Is anything wrong?"

Jake could only shake his head for a few seconds. Then he found his voice. "I'm . . . fine." He swallowed and it hurt; his throat was painfully tight.

"Then we should hurry a little and catch up with the others," Mrs. Richards said. She was still studying his face. Jake stepped up his pace, wanting to get away from Mrs. Richards, away from her kindly concern. He liked her, but she had never been able to help him with Rob, and she sure wasn't going to be able to help him with this.

When he was a few steps ahead of Mrs. Richards,

Jake began trying to convince himself that everything was all right. "You're being silly," he whispered under his breath. "What you think is happening *can't* be happening. Reflections aren't separate beings with . . . faces. They . . . they just *reflect*."

He glanced back at Mrs. Richards. She was still looking at him, her forehead wrinkled. "If you need someone to talk to, Jake, you could see your counselor. It's Mr. Yin, right? Or Ms. Harring? You've seemed very tense in class lately. If anything is wrong—"

"I don't need to talk to anyone," Jake assured her. Had she heard any of what he'd said to himself? He could only hope not. He walked a little faster, feeling like a mad bomber in a movie, making his way through the crowd slowly enough that no one would really notice him, but fast enough to get away.

Jake turned into the library and headed for the table in the very back. Other kids had already stacked their stuff on it. He added his, then automatically scanned the room for Rob, who was nowhere to be seen. That meant Rob was in-between the shelves somewhere, or, if Jake was lucky, already on his way back to the room, carrying a bathroom pass from the librarian. Jake wished silently that he could be there to see Rob's face when he found out the classroom door was locked. At least one good thing had happened today.

As he sat in the library, Jake tried to calm down. He nodded at a couple of kids, saying hello as though everything was normal. After a few minutes he began to think it probably was. How could he have seen anything in something as blurry as a key ring or a spoon? Or seen something in a mirror that disappeared a split second later? He didn't need a counselor. He needed to figure out some way to make Rob Phillips leave him alone.

Mrs. Richards always let them stay in the library for a long time, and this morning was no different. Jake watched the door until Rob came back. When he came in he was humming, acting like everything in his life was just perfect. Had he gone back to the classroom? Jake couldn't tell.

"What are you going to do your report on?"

Jake turned to see Don Blair standing behind him. He was already carrying a stack of books. Jake read the first title. *Football: Basic Skills* was a slim red paperback. Don glanced down when he noticed Jake looking at it.

"I'm not sure Mrs. Richards will let me do a report on an instruction book, but I'm going to ask. Hey, I heard you let Rob have it this morning. Good for you."

Jake shook his head. "It'll probably just make him hate me more."

Don looked around, spotting Rob on the far side of the room. "I beat him once at Ping-Pong and it

39

ruined our friendship forever. Don't worry about him."

Jake tried to smile. That was easy for Don to say. Rob wasn't putting gelatin in his desk and ruining his homework.

"Let's all spend our time wisely, looking for books," Mrs. Richards said, from behind them. Don ducked his head and moved away without looking back. Two girls who had been whispering at the next table suddenly became very studious. Mrs. Richards looked at Jake.

"Have you found something yet?"

He shook his head and looked around. "No. I was just about to start looking."

Mrs. Richards smiled. "I see. Well, don't let me slow you down."

Jake walked between the shelves of books, turning a corner almost immediately so Mrs. Richards couldn't see that he was blushing. He liked reading; he liked the library. He had just been too preoccupied with Rob to do what he was supposed to be doing. He walked aimlessly between the stacks for a moment, then headed for the science fiction shelf.

There were some kids in front of him, blocking his view, but after a minute a few of them left and he could stand close enough to the shelf to read the titles. He was scanning them when he felt a scrape down the back of his ankle. He whirled around, expecting to find Rob standing right behind him, but Rob was nowhere to be seen. Then the sound of quiet laughter made Jake turn. Off to one side, Rob stood looking at him. The instant Jake faced him, Rob stopped laughing and moved away, looking like he'd just thought of the perfect book and knew exactly where to find it.

Jake turned back to the science fiction shelf, but he spent the rest of the library time expecting Rob to do something else, which meant he could hardly concentrate on the books in front of him. When the bell rang, he grabbed a novel he'd already read and liked and hurried to the checkout desk with it.

On the way back from the library, Jake slipped out of line and took the shortcut between the main school building and the cafeteria. That meant he got back to the room before anyone else. He was waiting by the door when Mrs. Richards unlocked it. He made a point of hurrying inside, too, so that he was sitting in his desk when Rob came in. As Mrs. Richards started their math lesson, Jake relaxed a little. At least Rob wouldn't get a chance to ruin his homework today if he was careful at recess.

After school, Jake started down the hall, feeling pretty good. Recess inside hadn't been so bad. Don Blair had had some math to make up. Once they'd both finished their work, Mrs. Richards had taken a checkerboard out of the storage room and they had played a game. Jake had won and Don had been polite about it. By the time the bell rang, Jake was almost relaxed—he'd nearly forgotten about the walk home. He thought about asking Don if they could walk home together, but then he hadn't. It would be embarrassing if Rob followed them, stepping on Jake's heels as he normally did. So, as usual, when the second the bell rang and Mrs. Richards dismissed them, Jake bolted for the door alone.

Rob was almost as fast. He followed Jake down the hall, stepping on the backs of his shoes so many times that Jake's ankles began to hurt. Jake spun around twice, but Rob just stepped to one side, his face blank, pretending complete innocence.

At the big double doors, Jake dodged sideways and managed to run down the steps fast enough so that Rob couldn't keep up. After that, Jake wove in and out of the crowd, not actually running, but moving pretty fast. He was used to this and he had gotten pretty good at it. After all, he did it nearly every day.

Jake started up the sidewalk, resisting the urge to turn and see if Rob was still trying to keep up. Sometimes Rob gave up; those were the good days. But as much as Jake wanted to know whether or not this was going to be a good day, he didn't turn around to see if Rob was there or not. Usually, if Jake made eye contact at all, Rob would use the opportunity to insult him or make fun of him somehow. Jake kept his pace even, expecting every second the rough scrape of Rob's shoe down his ankle and heel. But they reached the end of the first block and it hadn't come. Jake began to hope.

He walked a little faster, passing a group of girls. "I heard about what you said to Rob Phillips this morning," one of them said as he passed. "Good for you." Jake smiled at her, but he didn't slow down. He knew a lot of kids thought Rob was a pain, and it made him feel a little better. But only a little.

At his corner, Jake turned. The crowd thinned out—most of the kids went straight. Jake took a deep breath. Usually, if he made it to his corner without Rob catching up, he was home free. Rob didn't turn here. He went straight for another two blocks, then turned up his own street.

Jake slowed his step, feeling the tension leaving his shoulders and neck. The afternoon was warm and the air still had that clean, washed feeling from the rain over the weekend. Even the old eucalyptus trees that lined the sidewalk looked fresh, not dusty, like they usually did. Jake walked along, enjoying the smell of the trees and the warmth of the afternoon. For a second he remembered what life was like without Rob Phillips: it was wonderful. There were a few kids walking nearly a block ahead of him. He almost had the whole street to himself.

Jake slowed a little more, noticing a restored, polished old car parked by the curb. The fenders were sea green, rounded and smooth, like an old-fashioned toaster. It was a beautiful car and Jake stopped to admire it. Whoever took care of it was obviously really proud of it.

"You jerk." The voice was so low and so close that Jake flinched. "You're gonna be sorry."

Jake didn't even have time to brace himself before Rob shoved him. He stumbled off the curb and fell, ending up half in the gutter, his nose almost touching the rear tire of the shiny old car. He wriggled around, trying to get up, raising his chin a few inches.

What Jake saw made him forget about Rob. There, in the shiny surface of the polished hubcap, was the reflection guy, the mirror man. He was smiling and his face got bigger, as though he was moving closer. Then he winked.

Jake looked away, then looked back, blinking. The mirror man was still there, and he was smiling. "Don't worry about this bully," the mirror man whispered. "You and I will take care of him."

Jake swallowed hard, staring into the shining, curved surface, seeing only his own startled face now. He rolled onto his side, then sat up. How could a reflection talk? He felt his pulse race, and a film of sweat sprang out on his forehead. Reflections didn't talk. Jake felt like the whole world had been turned upside down and no one had bothered to tell him about the change.

"Get up."

Startled, Jake looked up, squinting against the slanting sunlight. Rob was standing on the sidewalk.

"Get up and fight."

Jake shook his head. "I don't want to fight you. I just never want to see you again."

"Are you afraid?"

Jake glanced back at the hubcap, wishing Rob would leave so he could think about what was happening to him. "Yes," he said, "but not of you."

"Afraid you'd get in trouble with your mommy?"

Just then the door of the house they were in front of opened and a man with gray hair came out onto the lawn. "Will you boys play somewhere else, please? I'm afraid one of you will scratch the car. I've put in a lot of time on that old Pontiac." His voice was pleasant. He seemed like a nice, reasonable man. "Boys? Please?"

Rob shot one last ugly frown toward Jake and muttered something under his breath. Then he walked away, back toward the corner. A few seconds later the man nodded politely at Jake and went back into his house.

Careful not to even glance at the hubcap, Jake stood up slowly, slapping at the sand and dirt on his clothes. He waited until his breathing had evened out, then looked down at the polished hubcap. The only reflection in it now was of the gray-green tree branches arching overhead.

"Thanks," the man called from inside his screen door, and Jake knew he was only waiting for him to leave. Jake nodded and started home, his heart still thudding against his ribs.

5

For the next few days, Rob actually left Jake alone—sort of, anyway. He still stepped on the backs of Jake's shoes in the hall, and he made fun of Jake once when he dropped his pencil. But there were no special tricks—no gelatin, no dog poop, no dead bugs in his books. For Jake, it would have been almost like having a vacation, except that now he had to worry even more about the mirror man.

The afternoon the mirror man had spoken to him, Jake had gone home, shut himself in his room, and spent about an hour thinking. He tried to find some explanation for the mirror man, but of course there wasn't one—not one that made any sense. He was starting to believe that the mirror man was real, though, and *that* was scarier than thinking he'd imagined everything.

If he was real, what did he want? What had he meant when he'd said he and Jake could take care of Rob? Jake shivered every time he thought about

46

the mirror man. He tried to stay away from anything shiny. He walked past the old car with the chrome hubcaps every day on the way to school and again on the way home. He kept his eyes straight ahead when he got close, and he walked fast. But every time he had to do it, his heart pounded as if he'd been running.

Jake wanted to tell someone about the mirror man, but he couldn't imagine anyone believing him; he was having trouble believing it himself. But somehow he knew it wasn't just something he was imagining because he was upset about Rob and tired of his sisters' noise and silliness. He might have imagined the mirror man's face, but not his voice, not the words he had spoken.

But, Jake told himself over and over, just because the mirror man was real didn't mean he ever had to talk to him—or see him again, if he was just careful enough. And if he could avoid the mirror man until he gave up and went away, then he would never have to try to tell anyone about him, either.

Thursday morning, as Jake was getting ready for school, the twins were running up and down the hall, Becca starting at one end, Tracy at the other. When they met in the middle, they'd scream and pretend to circle each other like airplanes in a dogfight, their arms out like wings.

Jake made his way around them and went into

47

the bathroom. At this hour of the morning, it was still pretty dark. In one swift motion he flipped the light switch on, then off, his eyes on the mirror. In the quick flash of light he could see that the mirror was empty except for the things that should be there—reflections of the shower curtain and the silly picture of a clown his mother had hung above the towel rack on the far wall.

Jake breathed a little more slowly and flipped the light back on. Usually, if the mirror man was going to be there, he was there from the moment Jake glanced at something. Not always, though. So Jake hurried. He turned the light on again just long enough to run a comb through his hair. Then he turned it off while he was brushing his teeth.

The instant he was finished, he was out the door and on his way downstairs. In the kitchen he faced away from the glass oven door and the toaster and the shiny faucet.

"I made French toast this morning," his mother said, smiling.

Jake smiled back at her. He almost felt normal. It had been several days since Rob had bothered him very much and just as long since he'd seen the mirror man. He was beginning to hope he'd never see the mirror man again. Maybe he'd found someone else to bother. It was possible. After all, he must have been somewhere doing something before Jake had seen him for the first time.

"Syrup or jam?"

"Jam." Jake stretched and yawned as his mother filled a glass with cold milk and brought his plate to the table. He glanced up at her as she set it down. Usually he made his own breakfast on school days.

"You are perhaps wondering why I'm waiting on you like this?" His mother grinned at him as he nodded. "I'm doing it because I realize that we spend very little time together lately. And I've been wanting to ask you a question." Jake looked down at the French toast. Had she noticed that he never wanted to look toward the counter top and always sat facing the door? Had she noticed him flicking the lights in the bathroom on and off?

She pulled out a chair and sat down beside him. Then she reached out and touched his arm. "I wondered if Rob was still bothering you at school."

Relieved, Jake looked up at her. "Not as much."

"Really?" His mother looked pleased. "Good. See? If you ignore a bully long enough, he'll usually give up. It isn't fun for them anymore if you don't react."

Jake nodded. Maybe it was true with most bullies, but Rob was above average in the bully department. In fact, he was downright gifted. It seemed to Jake that things had gotten better since he'd insulted Rob about the dog poop smell—and had been knocked down. Maybe that would be enough of a fight for Rob. Rob might be able to tell himself that he'd won and give it up now.

"Well, I'm glad to hear he's finally leaving you

alone. It was worrying me." Jake's mother got up. She started humming as she cleaned up the breakfast mess. Jake turned to smile at her and saw a flash of movement reflected in the black microwave door. He looked away, his smile fading. He finished his breakfast quickly, thanked his mother, and left the kitchen. It really was one of the worst places—practically everything in it was shiny.

Saturday morning Jake woke up early to the sound of the twins arguing just outside his door. It took him a moment to realize that it wasn't a school day.

"I want it!" Becca shouted.

"It's *my* turn," Tracy answered, just as loudly.

Jake frowned and closed his eyes again. The twins kept going.

"No, it isn't. It's *mine*."

"Nooooo!" Tracy sounded like a train whistle in an old movie.

"Keep your voices down. Your brother is trying to sleep." That was his mother. Jake appreciated her effort, but he also knew it wouldn't do any good. It didn't.

"Get away, Becca."

"No—*you* get away."

Jake pulled his pillow over his head. Today he had to get away from his sisters. Maybe he would call someone and go for a bike ride, or something. But who? How could he have friends? No one wanted to get on Rob's victim list. Don Blair was always nice to him, but that would mean playing football down at the vacant lot—that was where Don always spent Saturday mornings.

Jake shook his head, pressing his face into his pillow, thinking about it. There were a few kids he said hello to in the hall, a few who smiled at him sometimes. But the truth was, everyone pretty much avoided contact with him, and he couldn't blame them. He was pretty new at school, after all, so it wasn't like they were abandoning him—they had just never gotten to know him.

Jake grimaced, burrowing deeper into the pillow, even though it was getting harder to breathe. He felt like hiding, like finding something to wriggle under and never coming out. It wasn't fair. Rob was ruining the whole school year for him. The twins never gave him a moment's peace. And now there was the mirror man. Jake squeezed his eyes shut so tightly that he saw sprays of color inside his eyelids. He had to do something. He had to figure out a way to make things better.

Jake listened. The girls had gone downstairs. He uncovered his face and took a few deep breaths. He could still hear them, but the sound was much fainter now. It was almost quiet enough to think. He had a lot to think about, too, but he didn't want to. This morning, he just wanted everything to be normal.

He swung his feet to the floor and stood up. It

took about two minutes to get dressed. Then he hesitated at his door. Once he opened it, he'd be fair game for his sisters. They knew they couldn't wake him up, but once he was awake, there was no stopping them. Well, he was sick of wondering if every move he made was going to involve his sisters, Rob, or the mirror man.

Jake strode down the hall, his head high. He was going to do whatever he wanted to do today, and no one was going to stop him. He went into the bathroom and flipped on the light. He glanced at the mirror, sure it would be empty, as it had been all week. It wasn't.

His pulse hammered, speeding up so fast that he almost felt sick.

"Close the door," the mirror man whispered, "so we can talk."

Jake took a step backward, unable to stop staring into the mirror. His hand patted the wall, frantically searching for the light switch. Finally he found it. He flicked it off, still unable to turn or to stop staring at the mirror. When the room went dark, the mirror man disappeared. Jake stood, breathing hard, trying to make sense of what was happening. Maybe it was time to do something, instead of running away all the time.

Jake took four or five deep breaths and braced himself. He flicked the light back on. Instantly, the mirror man was there, smiling his weird, crooked smile. "Come in, Jake," he said reasonably. "Shut the door."

Jake felt his courage fading. What could he *do* about a weird being who lived in mirrors? "Leave me alone," he managed to say. The mirror man only smiled and raised one hand, crooking his index finger at Jake.

"I want to tell you something."

Jake shook his head, willing himself to turn out the light, to run, but he couldn't seem to do either one. The mirror man winked at him. "Just come in. I want to explain something to you."

"Jaaake!"

Becca pummeled the backs of Jake's legs. A second later, Tracy ran into Becca. Jake struggled to keep his balance. He managed to stay upright, more or less, and he lurched back toward the bathroom door.

The mirror man smiled and shrugged, then winked once more. Jake reached out and hit the light switch, turning to nudge the twins along. Had they seen the mirror man? They were giggling madly, poking at each other. They wouldn't have noticed if an elephant had been reflected in the mirror. Jake got them started toward the stairs and tried to keep them moving in a straight line. He wanted them as far away from the mirror as possible. *He* wanted to be as far away from it as he could get.

Downstairs, Jake's parents were talking about

what to do with the day. Jake looked out the window, paced across the kitchen for a glass of juice from the fridge, then slouched into one of the kitchen chairs. The twins arranged themselves on either side of him, playing a game of slap-and-flinch across his legs.

Jake's mother came over. "Good morning, Jake. Girls, leave your brother alone." Her voice was tired, as though she knew the twins wouldn't listen to her. They didn't.

Jake tried to look normal, but he knew he wasn't pulling it off when his mother focused on him, studying his face. "Jake? Is something wrong?"

He shook his head. His father looked up from the newspaper. "Want to go to the park and throw a softball around today?"

Jake started to shake his head again, but he stopped himself in time. Usually, he loved doing things like that with his father. If he refused, his mother would be sure something was wrong. It was, of course, but it wasn't anything he could tell his parents about. They either wouldn't believe him, or . . . Jake looked down at the twins, pretending to join in their hand-grabbing game while he tried to think.

He wasn't quite sure why he didn't want to tell his parents about the mirror man, but he didn't. He had no idea what they would do if he did tell them. What could they do? Make him go to a counselor, probably. And that wouldn't help at all. He wasn't sure why he was seeing the mirror man, but he was pretty certain he wasn't imagining it now. Whatever the mirror man was, he was real, and Jake had a strange feeling that it was his job to protect his family from the weird, crooked smile and the intense eyes.

"Jake?"

Jake snapped out of his thoughts. He looked at his father for a few seconds before he recalled what he'd asked him. Then he nodded.

"Sure, Dad. That'd be great."

His father stood up. "Give me five minutes to get ready."

When they got to the park it was sunny; it was going to be another unseasonably warm day. Jake's father was in a good mood; he was whistling. He parked near a wide expanse of green lawn that rimmed the little lake in the center of the park. Palm trees grew close to the water, leaning away from each other to get as much sun as possible. There were a few other families. Jake heard a woman on the other side of the lake calling for her kids. Her voice was shrill, impatient.

"Here we go," Jake's father said, sticking the key into the trunk lock. He opened it and reached in. Jake glanced around again. Nothing shiny, no reflective surfaces at all, here in the park. Only green, clean grass and wide-open space. He inhaled as big a breath as he could hold, then blew it out slowly. Maybe he could just forget about the mirror man here—at least for a little while.

"Jake?"

His father was holding a softball and two gloves, awkwardly trying to close the trunk. Jake reached to take the gloves, letting out the last of his deep breath as his father slammed the trunk closed. "Ready to play some catch?"

Jake nodded, actually meaning it. He jogged away from the car, tossing his father a glove. The sun was in his eyes and he missed his father's first throw, but he caught three after that, then a fourth.

"Get farther back," his father called. "Make it a little bit of a challenge."

Jake nodded and backed up. The woman across the lake had gone. Now there was a big, noisy family picnic starting up close to the water. They had a dozen little kids and three big dogs. Jake's father was pounding his fist into the pocket of his baseball glove. "Leather's stiff," he called. "We should do this more often."

Jake nodded and stood waiting. Across the little lake he could hear someone whistling for the dogs. There was a deep-throated bark mixed in with the shrieks of running children. Jake glanced across the water.

"Heads up," Jake's father called. Jake's attention snapped back to the ball, but his father had already thrown it. Before he could get his hand up or step aside, the ball was right in his face, smacking into his cheekbone.

Jake's father was beside him so fast it was hard to believe he'd been standing thirty feet away just a second before.

"You okay?"

Jake nodded. "It hurts pretty bad."

"But your eye . . . ?"

Jake nodded again. "Fine. It'll probably turn black and blue." He blinked elaborately, squinting at the ground, then up at the sky. Nothing was blurry. His eye just hurt, that was all. It had been a pretty hard throw. "We can play again in just a minute," Jake told his father.

"Okay. Or we could just walk around the lake for a while."

Jake touched his cheekbone and nodded. "Yeah. Okay."

Jake's father slid the softball into the pocket of his baggy shorts, and then they walked slowly around the little lake in silence, making a wide circle around the noisy family gathering by the shore. He checked Jake's eye three or four times, peering into the pupil. Finally they were back at the car.

"We could take you to Dr. Balen."

Jake shook his head. "Nah, Dad. I'm fine."

His father's face was tight, worried. "It's turning pretty red."

Jake blinked again, testing his vision. He could

57

focus on the farthest point he could see, a red car parked on the hill across from them, above the lake. He looked up at the sky. The clouds looked normal. He looked at his own hand close up. He could see the convoluted ridges that made his fingerprints.

"I can see fine, Dad."

Jake's father reached into the car and flicked open the glove compartment. He pulled out something Jake recognized instantly. His heart began to speed up a little. "It's okay, Dad," he said uneasily.

"But here, take a look," his father insisted, passing him the little mirror Jake's mother used sometimes to comb her hair in the car.

Jake took the mirror, but his father had to lift his hand for him. "Jake, take a look. I think we should go see Dr. Balen just to be safe."

Jake shook his head, but his father pushed the mirror a little higher, making an impatient sound deep in his throat. "Just take a look, Jake."

Jake fought an urge to knock the mirror out of his father's hand. He took a deep breath instead and looked into it. He saw exactly what he knew he was going to see.

There was his own face, with his eye blood-red, his cheekbone and eyebrow bruised and swelling, and peeking out over Jake's shoulder, as though he was somehow standing behind him, was the mirror man. Maybe, Jake thought, I should get Dad to look, let him see the mirror man, too.

"It won't work, Jake," the mirror man whispered.

58

"It's all right. He can't see me. You don't have to worry about that. And you won't tell. That would be stupid, wouldn't it?" The mirror man's voice was low and a little . . . threatening.

Jake swallowed hard and pretended to check out his eye while he tried to understand what was going on. Was the mirror man reading his thoughts? He cleared his throat, suddenly aware that his father was staring at him, waiting for him to say something.

"It looks pretty bad, Dad," Jake said finally. "But it isn't. Really. We don't need Dr. Balen for this."

"He can't hear me, either," the mirror man went on, winking at Jake. "You want to get back at him for hitting you like that? Are you mad about it?"

Jake lowered the mirror. Either the mirror man had stopped whispering, or Jake couldn't hear him unless he was looking at him. It had been bad enough *seeing* the mirror man everywhere. Now that he was talking, it was terrible. How could Jake act normally? How could he feel normal?

Jake turned a little, pretending to face the sun for better light to see his stinging, bloodshot eye. "Go away," Jake whispered at the mirror. "Leave me alone."

"What?" Jake's father asked, his voice heavy with concern. "What are you saying?"

Jake shook his head. "Nothing. It just hurts, that's all." That much was true. His whole cheek stung and ached.

His father was looking at him closely. "I'm sorry this happened, Jake—really sorry. Are you sure that you can see fine?"

"I bet he isn't really sorry," the mirror man said. He nodded knowingly at Jake. "I bet you could make him sorry. With a little help from me, that is."

"Perfect," Jake said. "I can see just perfect." He nodded again, lowering the mirror until it hung at his side. It felt too warm. Or maybe his hands were too warm, sweaty. His father took the mirror back and leaned into the car to toss it back in the glove compartment. "Want to go get some pancakes somewhere?"

Jake nodded, trying hard to think about pancakes, about anything but the ugly little man in the mirror. How *dare* he suggest Jake would want to get even with his father for an accident? The mirror man was evil, that much Jake knew for sure. He was sure of one other thing, too. He was going to have to figure out a way to get rid of the mirror man.

Jake was a little late leaving for school the next morning. He had combed his hair without looking in a mirror, so when his mother made a big fuss over his black eye, he was a little surprised.

"It looks terrible," she kept saying. "Oh, Jake, it must hurt."

The truth was, it did hurt. It hurt a lot. But he still didn't want to go look at it in a mirror. In fact, he wanted to get out of the kitchen. There were too many reflective surfaces. The toaster was too shiny, the counter tops were always polished clean; you could see faint reflections in them. The black microwave door was shiny and Jake refused to look at it. He tried to concentrate on his cereal and toast— without looking directly at his butter knife. He pushed it beneath the edge of his plate.

"Morning, Jake," his father said. Jake looked up and saw him wince a little. "Boy. Well, it looks worse today. You can still see fine?"

Jake closed his good eye and looked across the room. Before he could catch himself, he glanced at the microwave. There, in the black rectangle, he saw a quick movement. Before he had time to blink, to look away, he saw the faint outline of the mirror man's face. The black surface cut down on detail, but Jake was sure. He looked down at his cereal.

"Jake?" The worry in his father's voice brought him back to reality. "Is your vision all right? If not—"

"It's fine," Jake interrupted. "Just fine. I can see perfectly."

He heard his father exhale with relief, but he didn't look up again. He ate his cereal, stood up, crossed the kitchen with his bowl, and set it in the sink, catching another glimpse of the mirror man in the shiny chrome faucet. He turned quickly and went out.

"You sure you're okay?" Jake's mother followed him to the front door. "Your father really feels terrible about this."

"Sure, I'm okay," Jake said, trying to sound insulted that she would even ask. He knew instantly that his tone of voice would only convince her that there was something wrong. He looked at his mother and forced a smile.

For the twentieth time he thought about telling her about the mirror man. And the moment he thought it, he knew he couldn't. He wasn't sure why. He imagined himself trying to explain and

62

winced. Abruptly he realized that he was afraid to tell anyone. Not just cautious or embarrassed or concerned that no one would believe him, or something—he was *afraid*.

Once he was out the door, Jake walked fast, keeping his eyes on the sidewalk before him. It was another too-hot, too-dry desert wind day. The rain had dried up completely. He scanned the crowd ahead of him when he turned the corner and joined the clusters of kids making their way to school.

Jake saw kids looking at him twice, noticing his black eye. He tried walking on the edge of the sidewalk with his head turned slightly toward the street, but after a while the crowd thickened and it was hard to keep from zigzagging through the groups of girls who were standing talking. He spotted Rob once, then lost him again close to the playground gate.

Somehow Jake made it all the way to class before Rob found him. The bell hadn't rung yet and kids were still milling around, out of their seats. Mrs. Richards was sitting at her desk, her attention focused on a stack of assignment papers.

Rob swaggered over to Jake's desk. Jake lifted his chin. There wasn't much point in trying to hide his black eye. In fact, he hoped Rob would tease him about it here, where Mrs. Richards and the presence of the other kids would keep him from getting too obnoxious.

"Fall down?" Rob asked.

Jake shook his head, disgusted at the glee in Rob's voice. Rob was actually enjoying the idea that he was hurt.

"What happened? Were you walking home and a tree decided to leap in front of you and you were going too fast to stop in time?" Rob asked.

"No," Jake informed him in a tight voice. "My dad and I were playing catch—"

"Oh. I get it. And you didn't," Rob finished for him. "Your dad must really like you a lot. Throwing that hard—and straight at your face. Well, I can't say that I blame him much. I—"

The final bell rang and Rob frowned. Mrs. Richards looked up, scanning the room.

"In your seats, please, everyone."

Rob started back toward his desk. Jake watched him go, anger flaring in his chest like a fire out of control. He'd like to give Rob two black eyes. Then maybe he'd shut up for a few days, at least. Jake started to imagine Rob melting like the gelatin had that day.

"Notebooks, please," Mrs. Richards said, interrupting Jake's fantasy. "I want you to take history notes today. Let's make sure everyone has a pencil or pen and plenty of clean paper before I start."

The room erupted into shuffling and creaking noises as kids opened their desks and pawed through their stuff. Jake pulled his three-ring binder out of his desk and went to sharpen two pencils. As he waited in line, he thought about the mirror man.

There just had to be some way ~~appearing—to make him go away~~ ... appearing—to make him go away to ... stop

Jake got to the front of the line a~~n~~ ... pencils in the sharpener one at a time. ... his out the window as the little electric blades ~~red~~ and hummed. He avoided looking at the sharp~~d~~ itself—parts of it were chrome colored, shi~~n~~ enough to show a reflection.

When he got back to his seat, Jake reached for his binder, trying to think of a way to open it and take out a few sheets of paper without having to look into the flat silver spine that held the rings. As the class began to quiet down and Mrs. Richards stood to write on the blackboard, Jake sighed and flipped open the binder. He knew he would see the mirror man, and he did. What he didn't expect was how loud the mirror man's voice could sound.

"Jake? We need to talk," the mirror man said. His eyes were so intense it was hard to break contact once it had been made. "I'm running out of patience," the mirror man went on. "You'd better stop trying to avoid me and listen. I can do something for you. I can help with—"

Jake dragged his eyes away from the mirror man's piercing gaze, and the instant he did, the voice stopped. Jake watched Mrs. Richards for a few seconds, trying to calm his breathing. Then, without really meaning to, he let his eyes slide back to the binder.

"You have to listen to me, Jake. I'm not going

ith this much longer. You think that
to
y ooked back at Mrs. Richards. The mirror
voice was so loud. Why couldn't anyone else
him? Why wasn't everyone in the classroom
ned toward him, wondering where the voice was
coming from?

Fumbling, without looking, he snapped the
binder rings open and lifted a sheet of paper out of
the notebook. Then he pushed the rings closed and
shut the notebook, all without glancing at it again.

"During the Civil War," Mrs. Richards was saying, "businesses and farms—left untended when
the men of both sides became soldiers—often had
to be taken over and run by women and children
not much older than you are. Some of them were
your age, or even younger." Jake started writing,
but his mind was elsewhere.

If the mirror man couldn't talk unless he was
looking at him, all Jake had to do was avoid anything that could hold a reflection. He sighed. Great
idea, he congratulated himself. Certainly a new ap-
proach. It was exactly what he'd *been* doing, and it
was hard—too hard. One of these days the mirror
man was going to catch him off guard someplace
he couldn't leave. And Jake wasn't sure what would
happen then. But he had a heavy feeling of dread.
He was sure that whatever the mirror man wanted
to talk about, it would end up being bad. Maybe
someone would even get hurt.

Jake felt an uncomfortable rush of anger. He was getting tired of all this. He just wanted to be left alone. All he wanted in the whole world was for Rob to stop bullying him, for the twins to give him a little more time to himself, and most of all, for the mirror man to disappear and never come back.

Mrs. Richards hit her desk lightly with her pointer. Jake's thoughts were scattered as he heard the sharp tapping sound. She went on with the history lesson. "These women and children adapted to new work during the Civil War because they had to," Mrs. Richards said. "It was hard for them at first, but they rose to the challenge—necessity forced them to learn quickly, and they did."

Jake stared out the window. He could see cars on the street, flashing by. The sun was bright, and he thought for an instant that he could see the mirror man reflected in a car window.

"You can," a voice whispered. It sounded as though the mirror man was standing beside him, leaning down to speak into his ear. Jake saw another flash of light reflected from someone's windshield. Within it was a familiar silhouette.

"What's wrong? Why won't you listen to me, Jake?"

Jake forced his attention back to Mrs. Richards. She was talking now about a woman who had run a hospital during the Civil War—General Lee had made her a soldier so she could keep the job. "But she refused," Mrs. Richards said, "because she felt it was improper for her to receive an honor that most men earned by fighting."

Jake tried to pay attention. Just then a tiny wad of paper hit his cheek. He brushed it away. A second wad hit him and rolled down into his lap. He turned just in time to see Rob smile. He caught a glimpse of something bright red in Rob's right hand and grimaced.

Oh, good. Rob had gotten hold of a plastic straw, so he was in a spitball-launching mood today. Well, well. How wonderful. Jake looked back at his notes. He made himself listen and tried to keep up. Mrs. Richards turned to write something on the board.

A third spitball bounced off Jake's cheek. He refused to look at Rob. If he did, he knew Rob would smile his nasty smile and then there would be another fifty spitballs before the day was over. Of course, if he ignored him, there would only be forty-nine.

Jake made himself concentrate on his notes, flipping the paper over to write on the back. Mrs. Richards was really interesting. He liked the way she explained things. She turned to underline something on the board. As soon as her back was to the class, a fourth spitball landed, almost in his ear this time. It was wet and sticky.

Jake felt like screaming out loud. How could someone like Rob get away with being such a jerk? Why couldn't anyone ever make him stop? Jake came to the end of his sheet of paper and flipped open his binder to take out another.

There, in the metallic spine of the notebook was the mirror man. He was smiling, as though Jake was someone who had dropped by unexpectedly for a visit. He was standing with his arms crossed, casually leaning to one side of the silver spine the way a person might lean against the side of a building.

"You want Rob to stop bothering you? How badly do you want that, Jake?" the mirror man whispered. His face and shoulders were rounded, distorted by the shape of the metal. Jake stared. The mirror man was reflected in each of the three rings, too, his face tiny and misshapen, spread around the curves of the rings. "Don't you want to know how?" The mirror man whispered the question. All of his faces spoke at once, their mouths moving in perfect unison.

Another spitball hit Jake's cheek. This one was really wet. It stuck to his skin, and before he could think about what he was doing, he impatiently slapped it away. Then he gasped. He had forgotten how tender the bruise beneath his eye was. His eye and cheek stung for a few seconds, then began to ache fiercely. Involuntarily he made a little sound of pain.

Jake heard Rob's smothered laughter and he gripped the edge of his desk top to keep from leaping up and hitting him. When his eye stopped throbbing and his anger settled a little, Jake looked back at the mirror man.

"You do want him to stop?"

Jake nodded slowly. "How?"

"Does anyone have any questions?" Mrs. Richards was saying. Jake looked up, and as he did, he felt like a weight had been taken from his heart. Without looking back at the binder, and before the mirror man could answer, Jake closed the notebook. His heart was racing and his palms were sweaty.

7

Walking home that day, Rob caught up and followed Jake almost all the way to his turnoff. He didn't say much, for a change, but he walked close enough to step on the backs of Jake's shoes a few times. Once Jake stumbled a little and Rob laughed, but when Jake ignored him, he got quiet again. Finally, Jake turned off and Rob went on, whistling softly to himself as he walked past Jake's street, heading toward his own.

You'll see, Jake heard himself thinking. *You'll find out who you should play tricks on and who you shouldn't.* Jake slowed his pace, realizing that he had almost made a decision. Maybe he *should* talk to the mirror man. Maybe he should find out how to stop Rob from making his life awful. Jake took a deep breath, feeling a prickling sensation in his scalp. Did he really want to talk to the mirror man?

"Yes," he whispered to himself. "I think I do." He looked down the street. All of a sudden, everything seemed to shine. There were dozens of windows, puddles from lawn sprinklers, glittering chrome on the cars. He could talk to the mirror man right now, if he wanted to.

An eruption of high-pitched laughter behind him startled Jake out of his thoughts. There were several girls ahead of him on the sidewalk and more behind. He looked back at the giggling group of girls and wondered what they would think if they saw him lying on his stomach, talking to a hubcap. No . . . he would wait.

Jake slowed his steps a little more. The easiest place to have a talk with the mirror man would be in the upstairs bathroom at home. He could lock the door and keep out the twins—and his parents. He felt his pulse speeding up as he thought about it. This was all pretty strange, but he was going to do it. It was either that or spend the rest of his life like this, scared and upset and wondering what to do about it.

After trying to avoid the mirror man for so long, the decision to talk to him seemed to lift Jake's spirits. He walked home with long strides, feeling better than he had since that Saturday morning in the kitchen when he'd been staring into his cereal spoon.

"Jaaake!" Becca called out, when she saw him. She and Tracy had a pile of blankets on the lawn. He could see their enormous collection of dolls sitting in two rows, facing each other. As he got closer,

he saw Tracy reach out to knock over three or four of the biggest dolls.

"Don't," Becca screamed. "They have to sit up or they can't see the parade."

Tracy looked sullen and got to her feet. "It's a stupid parade."

"It is not," Becca argued. "It has horses."

Jake veered a little, hoping the girls would be so absorbed in arguing about their fantasy parade that they wouldn't notice him passing. But of course, it didn't work that way. Tracy was already standing up, obviously getting bored with the game. She came barreling across the grass and fell into a half-trot beside him to keep up.

"Jake?"

He went up the steps before he turned to answer her. She was right behind him, her little mouth in a pout. "Jake? Guess what?"

Jake looked at her. "What?"

Tracy stuck her lower lip out even farther. "Your eye looks purple, like grape juice. It's kind of ugly, Jake."

Jake tried to smile at her. "I know, Tracy."

Tracy grabbed at his sleeve. "Guess what?"

"I did, Trace. Now I'm going to go up to my room." Tracy hung onto his sleeve. He had to pry her fingers loose. Her face was turning pink. She grabbed his shirt this time.

"Hi, Jake," he heard his mother call. "Good day at school?"

73

He mumbled some kind of answer and made his way around Tracy, working her fingers loose with his left hand and opening the screen door with his right. "I'll guess more later," he said, hoping she wouldn't start crying. Becca was yelling something, still talking about their pretend parade. Tracy looked across the lawn at her sister.

In that instant, Jake nearly leaped through the doorway. His mother had gone back into the kitchen. She was sitting at the table, where she could keep an eye on the twins through the window. The newspaper was spread out in front of her. "I might have to work tonight," she said, as he walked in. He started to protest.

"I was assured that this won't happen once they get the shifts worked out, Jake." She patted the newspaper. "If they ever do. I'm not sure I like this new manager they've hired. I'm looking, just in case."

"Really?" Jake realized the newspaper was open to the want ads. His mother had worked at Bellencamp's restaurant for as long as he could remember. He knew everyone there; he knew the owner, a nice elderly man with a ton of white hair. It would be weird if his mother worked somewhere else. But she was nodding. "The new manager keeps asking me to pick up the dinner shift. You know how much I hate it."

Jake nodded. His mother wanted to be home in the evenings, when his father was. She liked having dinner with her family, watching TV with the

74

twins, and helping him with homework if he needed it. But her job—

"I feel pushed around sometimes," his mother said, interrupting his thoughts. She sighed. "I guess I just get tired of other people running my life."

Jake nodded, understanding her perfectly. He waited a few seconds to see if she was going to say anything else. She tipped her head to one side. "Your eye looks a little better," she said. "Does it still hurt?" He shook his head, refusing to get into a conversation. His mother smiled at him. She looked out the window and checked on the twins, watching them for a minute. Then she looked back down at the want ads.

Jake waited another ten seconds or so, then hitched his backpack higher on his shoulders. "Guess I'll go upstairs now." His mother nodded, glancing out the window again, then back at the newspaper.

Jake looked out at the lawn through the screen door as he came out of the kitchen. Across the yard, Tracy had gone over to see what Becca was doing.

Jake smiled. They wouldn't see him. He was safe. He headed for the stairs and took them two at a time. He slipped into his room and closed the door behind himself. He could hear his sisters' playful shrieks and giggles outside, but it was distant, almost pleasant.

It was only after he'd been standing alone in his room for a minute or two that Jake allowed himself to think about the mirror man. It had made sense to consider talking to the mirror man while he'd been so furious with Rob. But what about now?

He shrugged off his backpack and let it thud to the floor. In between the times when he saw the mirror man, the whole thing seemed impossible. Jake's eyes drifted toward the window—then back—to the glass-covered poster of Africa.

He felt a cold sweat form on his forehead. He took a long, deep breath. He could see the mirror man, sitting cross-legged on his bed. Jake's eyes jerked from the glass to the rumpled bedspread. Of course, there was no one there. That part of the reflection was normal. His bed was what *should* be reflected in a shiny surface. Slowly, deliberately, Jake looked at the glass again.

The image was faint, but he was sure he saw the mirror man frowning. He didn't speak. Maybe he couldn't unless the reflection was brighter or more distinct. Or maybe he just didn't feel like talking. Maybe he was angry. The thought made Jake's stomach tighten. Could the mirror man help him with Rob, somehow?

Jake took another deep breath and stood up. He glanced out the window. The twins were still play-ing happily on the lawn. He could hear his mother's radio downstairs. His father wouldn't be home for a couple of hours. Now was as good a time as any. He opened his door and headed down the hallway to the bathroom.

Jake went inside and closed the door. For a few moments he just stood there in the dark, listening to the sound of his own breathing. When he finally did turn on the light, he hit the switch so hard that he hurt the palm of his hand.

Instantly, as the room was flooded with light, Jake's reflection flashed to life, his eye purple and bloodshot. Behind him, the mirror man stood looking over his shoulder. Then, as Jake watched, his own image seemed to shimmer and step aside, leaving most of the room in the mirror for the mirror man.

The mirror man was smiling broadly, sitting cross-legged, hunched over, so that he filled the entire frame of the mirror over the sink. His face was oddly off balance, and his teeth looked too narrow, too long. But it was true that he looked something like Jake. Like a cousin, maybe, or a brother, or something. Jake shuddered. *A brother from another planet*. The mirror man was not human.

Well, no kidding, Jake heard himself thinking. Brilliant observation. If he was human, he wouldn't live in mirrors and hubcaps and notebooks. But what was he, then? Jake tried to ignore the slamming of his heart and the film of cold sweat that was prickling his skin.

As Jake watched, the mirror man unfolded his legs. He seemed to step down to stand on something behind the mirror. "Well. Hello at last, Jake."

The mirror man's voice was soft, almost gentle, but his eyes were hard and fierce looking. Jake could only stare. He pulled in a deep breath but only let it out again, unable to say anything at all. "I know this must be somewhat strange for you," the mirror man said.

Again Jake took a breath. But what could he say? The prickly feeling was back, crawling up his spine, resting for a moment on his neck, then sliding up his scalp and into his hair. It was creepy to be looking into a mirror and seeing someone else's face. No, not *someone* . . . more like some*thing*.

"You will get over this feeling."

Jake shook his head. "I doubt it. It's weird to have you read my mind, too. I don't know where you come from, but it sure as heck isn't this neighborhood." His voice was croaky, but at least he'd managed to say something. And it seemed to be very funny—at least, for the mirror man.

"Ah!" The mirror man began to laugh. It was an ugly, grating sound that made Jake want to cover his ears. "Ah," he repeated. "You are trying to make a joke."

Jake shook his head again. "Who . . . what *are* you?"

The mirror man arched his eyebrows. "That's an open debate."

Jake waited, trying to stay calm. In a way, the only sensible thing to do was to turn and run out the door. He glanced at it, imagining his hand on the doorknob. It sure would be easy to run away.

"Oh, no, don't do that, Jake. It'd be very foolish, very dangerous."

Jake felt the prickling start again, crawling faster this time. "Don't do what?"

"Leave. Run out and slam the door."

Jake felt a little sick. "How can you read my . . . read my—"

"Your thoughts are very much like my own. Jake, I've come to give you the power. Or rather, to tell you that you already have it. All you have to do is use it."

Jake swallowed. "Power . . ." He cleared his throat. *"Power?"*

The mirror man nodded and shifted around again until he seemed to be leaning into the mirror as if it were a camera lens. Now only his face showed, huge and close. "The power," he said slowly, "is the whole reason I am here. You can't refuse it, really. It is wiser not to try."

Jake shook his head. "I don't know what you're

79

talking about. I only did this because you said you could stop Rob—"

"No," the mirror man interrupted. "I said *we* could stop him. And we can. I have given you the power. You can do with it what you will." He smiled again, the corners of his mouth tipped upward like a painted clown's. "You. And me. That's *we*."

Jake stood without speaking. He had no idea what to say or do. This was like a puzzle with lousy clues—there was no way he could figure it out. After a moment, he heard his sisters' voices. Were they still out on the lawn? He couldn't tell which direction the sounds were coming from. Were they coming up the stairs, or just yelling at each other downstairs?

The mirror man was smiling. "You have a good imagination. You will enjoy the power. I know you will."

"What are you talking—" Jake began, but the mirror man had disappeared. The only face in the mirror now was his own. For the first time in a long time, Jake really studied his own image. In addition to the purple-black bruises on his eye, he looked pale and half sick . . . which was how he felt. "What power?" he asked the mirror.

The mirror remained empty. Jake could still hear the twins. They were getting louder now. He could hear the whumping and thudding that meant they were coming up the stairs.

"Jaaake?" It was Tracy's voice, and she sounded whiny. *"Jaaake?"*

Jake flinched as though someone had hit him. He wasn't sure his nervous system could stand up to a twin attack just now. If they started hitting each other and arguing, or screeching in their high, squeaky voices, he'd probably blow up at them. What a perfect expression that is, Jake thought. Blow up. Like a pressure cooker when the safety valve gets clogged. That was how he felt most of the time lately.

"Jaaake?" Tracy was at the door. "Come and play with us. We want to play Sharks. I can already see some coming!"

"Please, Jake?" That was Becca. She had a little whine in her voice, too. Jake clenched his fists. Why couldn't they just leave him alone for a little while? Why couldn't they?

"Jake?" This time it was his mother's voice. She sounded apologetic. "I have to take off pretty soon. They called. I'm sorry." He could tell she was upset, and he didn't want to upset her more. But this was the worst day ever to ask him to take care of the twins until Dad got home.

Jake stared into the mirror.

"You two go on and play in your room for a while, now," Jake could hear his mother saying. "Until your father comes home, I want you to be good and quiet and let Jake alone."

Becca said something, but Jake couldn't understand her words. Then the twins' voices got farther and farther away. After a few seconds, the hallway was very quiet.

"I have to get dressed for work now, Jake," his mother said from the other side of the door. "I'll say goodbye when I'm actually on my way. You're sure you're all right?"

"Sure," Jake called back. He turned on the sink faucet, counted to five, then turned it off again. Then, after a few seconds more, he turned it on again. He didn't hear his mother walk away, but he was sure she had.

Jake glanced in the mirror and saw the mirror man again. This time he was sitting in a position that made it look like he was perched on the mirror image of the counter. "It'll be fine," he whispered. "You're going to enjoy it." Jake's whole body reacted to the sound. He thought he saw a quick movement in the silvered glass, but he wasn't sure. Then the mirror man disappeared. Jake's own face stared back at him, still pale and sick looking.

"Jake? Answer, please. I have to get going." That was his mother again.

"Jaaake? Come and play." That was Becca.

Jake pictured the little crowd assembled on the other side of the door. It was almost funny, except that it wasn't. "I'll be out in a second," he yelled. "Just please give me a minute." He turned on the water in the sink, then leaned over to look into the mirror. "Are you there?" Jake whispered. His own face continued to stare out at him, but the mirror man was apparently gone. He took a deep breath. It was weird. For weeks now he'd been avoiding every mirror he could. Now he was staring into one and the mirror man wasn't there.

Jake clenched his hands into fists. The power . . . what did that mean? He tried squeezing his hands shut tightly, flexing his arms into a muscle pose. He didn't feel any stronger than usual. Or any smarter. Or any more of anything. Except lousy. He felt awful. He turned on the water again, this time to really splash his face.

"Jake?"

It was his mother. He turned off the water.

"I have to go now. You're sure you're okay?"

He could hear the concern in her voice. He knew she cared about him and was just worried. After all, he'd been acting pretty strangely. He opened the door a little. His mother was dressed for work.

"I have to get going, Jake. I'm really sorry about this."

He nodded. "It's . . ." He had to clear his throat. "It's all right, Mom."

She smiled at him. "I won't let it go on much longer. If they can't straighten out the schedules soon, I'll start looking seriously for another job."

Jake nodded. His mother was still smiling, but she looked worried.

"I'm all right," he told her, trying to smile back at her. It crinkled up his face and made his eye hurt. It was odd that he hadn't noticed that before—that smiling made his eye hurt. Maybe, Jake thought, I haven't been smiling very much lately.

"So, okay," his mother said, looking uncertain. "I'll see you tomorrow morning, then, I guess. Don't wait up for me. I won't be home until about eleven. Your father will be here in a couple of hours."

Jake nodded, wishing he could say something to make her feel better. But he couldn't. He could hear his sisters in their room, playing. His mother followed his glance and his thought.

"I told them to try to play in their room until their father got here." She shrugged, still smiling, studying his face. He could tell that she knew something was wrong but had no idea what it was. How could she?

"Maybe they'll play quietly until your dad comes home."

"That should last about twenty minutes," Jake said, and immediately felt guilty about sounding so nasty and sarcastic. He didn't want to babysit the twins, but he knew his mother couldn't help having to work. "It's okay," he added, and his voice still sounded resentful and mean, not at all the way he had intended.

"Are you coming out of there?" his mother asked.

Jake suddenly realized he was still hanging on to the bathroom door, talking to his mother through a ten-inch opening. He pushed his face forward so she could see him—and bumped his cheekbone, high, at the edge of his bruises. He grunted, startled at the sudden pain.

"I'm so sorry about your eye," his mother said, glancing at her watch. Jake opened the door halfway, feeling weird. He patted the wall, without looking, until he found the light switch. He turned off the light and tried to smile again as his mother said goodbye and rushed down the hall.

Jake stared at the empty hall for a few moments, feeling the presence of the mirror behind him as though someone were standing there. Well, the truth was that someone really *was* standing there. For a second, he even imagined that he could hear breathing.

Impulsively, he flicked on the light and leaned back into the bathroom, but the mirror man wasn't there. Jake saw his own face, bruises and all, looking confused and scared. He flipped off the light again.

Jake knew he had to figure out what to do about the mirror man. If he got lucky, the twins would stay out of his way for a while and give him a chance to think. He shook his head. Who was he trying to fool, himself? He felt a swell of fear. What was the power the mirror man was talking about?

Jake heard the twins erupt into giggles. At least they were getting along. They were usually a little tired this time of day. Often they fought as much as they played. He'd probably have to spend most of the next two hours trying to settle them down and make them get along with each other.

Jake stood very still in the darkened bathroom.

The giggles had stopped and he could hear the twins yelling. Of course. He listened as his sisters began shrieking at each other. It was loud even through the closed door of their room. Jake cringed, but he didn't move. Maybe if he just left them alone for a little bit, they would work out the argument on their own. They sometimes did.

He moved into the hallway and closed the bathroom door behind himself. He stood there for a second, looking toward the twins' closed door. They were still yelling.

He flinched as their high, shrill voices got even louder. He was kidding himself if he thought he was going to get any time to think. The twins wouldn't stay out of his way unless they somehow just disappeared. For a moment he pictured their room as serene, peaceful, and perfectly neat. He imagined it empty, without little girls to shriek in high, squeaky voices. He imagined the beds perfectly made, the toys all picked up for the first time ever. He enjoyed the mental image. It would be wonderful to have a nice, perfect, quiet, empty room at the end of the hall.

The twins' voices got louder and louder. They were really screaming at each other now. He clung to his imagined image, trying to tell himself that he had to go in and solve whatever argument they had gotten into now.

Abruptly the twins' voices stopped. Jake let out his breath in a soft, relieved sigh. Good. Better than good. It was amazing. He smiled and his bruises ached again, so he relaxed his face. The twins were so quiet that he could almost believe in the perfect empty room down the hall. At least he'd have a few minutes before the next argument erupted. Even a few minutes would be better than nothing.

Amazingly enough, the twins remained quiet and didn't come out of their room as Jake tiptoed down the hall. He silently opened his door and went into his room. If he was incredibly lucky, they'd think he was still in the bathroom and leave him alone a little longer.

But lying on his bed, Jake found that he couldn't really relax or think—with or without the twins' noise to distract him. His thoughts spun like a whirlwind. There was no logic to the mirror man's appearances or his weird claim that he had given Jake some kind of power.

Jake knew it had all happened; it was real. But he could just imagine trying to tell his parents—or anyone else, for that matter. They'd assume he was making it all up. Maybe he was. He rubbed his eyes. He felt so tired and confused—and scared. What would happen next? Would the mirror man come climbing out of the wall, or something? And if no one else could see or hear him . . .

Jake shivered. He sat up abruptly. Lying on his bed, listening to himself think, wasn't going to do him any good. He opened his backpack and took out his history book. He would just spend some time reading, doing his history homework, and try hard not to think about the mirror man.

He managed to do the work, but he couldn't seem to stop glancing at the glass covering the African poster. Every time he looked, his heartbeat quickened a little. But each time it was for nothing. He saw only an elongated reflection of his bed, himself, his chair, and his desk. The mirror man was apparently gone . . . at least for now.

He closed his history book. He felt restless, nervous. The whole experience of talking to the mirror man had left him feeling strange.

"Right," Jake said aloud, speaking to himself. "And how should it have left you feeling? Great? Happy? Full of fun?"

He realized suddenly that the twins had been quiet for too long. He got up and stretched. Time to go check on them. He glanced once more at the glass in the picture frame. Still empty. He felt an odd ache—like loneliness, or something. He shook his head. What was wrong with him? It wasn't like he missed the mirror man. It'd be the best thing in the world if he disappeared forever, wouldn't it?

"It sure would," Jake whispered.

He looked back over his shoulder from the doorway. The glass didn't reflect anything at this angle, just the lighted rectangle of his open door. If the mirror man never came back, maybe Jake *would* eventually convince himself he'd imagined the whole thing. It was probably possible. People made up all kinds of weird things in their minds. He took a deep breath. Maybe it was over. Maybe he would never see the mirror man again. But one thing was certain: he hadn't imagined it.

He walked quickly down the hall, then paused at the doorway to the twins' room. He hated to disturb them if they were just playing happily and quietly for a change. Once in a while they did. And if he opened the door, the minute they saw him they'd leap up, excited and squealing with eagerness to play with him.

Jake pushed open the door an inch and peeked in. The twins' room was oddly clean and organized. Their beds were made and there were no toys on the floor. Once in a while his mother got tired of their messes and cleaned everything up, but it usually didn't last this long. It took about five seconds for Jake to figure out why the twins had been quiet for a while. They were gone. But where would they go?

He pushed the door open wide. He took in a deep breath and glanced out the twins' window as he turned back down the hall. It was getting dusky outside. That meant it was about six o'clock. His father would be home pretty soon.

Jake jogged to the head of the stairs. "Becca?

Tracy?" There was no answer. They couldn't have left their room; he would've heard them—unless they had tried to sneak past, had tried to be quiet. Maybe they were back out on the lawn—but they'd have known he wouldn't let them go out this late in the evening. Jake shook his head. They wouldn't have gone outside without permission, he was pretty sure. Probably they were just downstairs.

Jake went down the stairs and ran into the living room. The twins weren't there. He flipped on the lights as he went into the kitchen. No twins. The toaster glittered and the chrome faucet shone in the bright light. No twins, and no mirror man. Jake swallowed, a vague feeling of dread weighing on his heart. He spun around abruptly and sprinted for the front door.

"Becca! Tracy?" Jake was yelling as he opened the front door. He ran to the edge of the porch, looking out over the lawn. The twins' mounds of blankets were still out there. He ran across the grass.

The dolls still sat side by side, their eyes fixed and empty in the dimming light. He poked at the blankets, then lifted them, sweeping them aside. The twins weren't here. Where were they? Hiding? Jake shook his head. He was sure going to be furious with them when he did find them. They were going to get a lecture, all right. They had no right to scare him like this. He could feel his heart thudding at his ribs. Where were they? Where were his sisters?

Jake hurried back into the house and went through the living room again, then the kitchen, then the laundry room. He glanced up the stairs. If they were hiding, they were upstairs somewhere.

"What if they aren't hiding?" Jake wondered aloud, and he felt his stomach tighten. He went up the stairs two at a time and looked into his room, then the bathroom, and finally the twins' room again. "Tracy?" He bent to look beneath her perfectly made bed. "Becca?" He looked under Becca's bed. Nothing.

He straightened up, sweat springing to his forehead. Where were they? Where could they possibly *be?* He took a step backward. It was time to call his mother, or 911, or something. He shouldn't just be standing here. He heard a distant thumping noise. He turned his head, trying to figure out where it was coming from.

"Oh, no," Jake whispered, when he'd figured it out. His father was home. He'd heard the car door shutting down below, in the driveway. He knew his father would help him find the twins—but now he was going to have to admit that he'd let them sneak out. Or maybe they *were* still hiding somewhere in the house.

He turned numbly and started for the stairs. If his father was home, it was six o'clock. His mother had left at four or four-thirty. How could he have neglected checking on the twins for so long? His father would open the front door any second now. Usually, Jake looked forward to that sound when he was babysitting the twins. Once his father came home, he was free to close himself in his room.

"Becca? Tracy?" Jake roared his sisters' names at the top of the stairs, hoping, wishing, that he'd hear an answer. But there wasn't one. Instead, the front door opened and his father came in.

"Hi, Jake," he said, smiling. "Mom called me. How's it going?"

Jake swallowed. "I lost . . . I lost the twins."

His father just stared at him for a few seconds. "You mean you don't know where they are?"

Jake nodded and watched his father's face go pale.

"For how long? How long ago did you see them? Where were they?"

His father started toward the stairs, then turned back. "Jake!" It was a shout. "Help me. When did you see them last?"

"When Mom left," Jake mumbled. Then he repeated it a little louder.

The color came back into his father's face, but Jake knew it was from anger. "When she *left?*"

Jake nodded again. "I just . . . I did my homework and they were quiet for a change and I just . . . I forgot to check on them."

Jake's father was shaking his head in disbelief.

93

"And you're sure they aren't in the house somewhere?"

Jake nodded. "Pretty sure. I've looked everywhere."

His father pounded up the stairs, calling the girls' names.

Jake stood for a second, then ran out the front door, looking wildly around the yard. No twins. He ran to the sidewalk, checking up and down the block. Nothing.

After a few minutes, he stood helplessly on the lawn, wondering what to do next. He could start knocking on the neighbors' doors or go and look in the vacant lot down the block. Sometimes the twins liked to play there. But they were never allowed to go on their own, and certainly not in the dark. He had to be there, or one of his parents.

Jake felt sick. He had been selfish, caught up in his own thoughts and problems and the crazy experience with the mirror man—and now his sisters were lost. *Lost.* Jake swallowed. He kept looking around, his eyes darting across the lawn, across the street, then back. He half expected his sisters to run giggling out of the hedge. But they didn't.

Jake could hear his father inside the house, calling the twins' names, his voice getting louder and louder, more and more frantic. He started back toward the front door just as his father flung it open and burst outside.

"Jake? Have you looked all over out here?"

He nodded, but his father went right past him, calling the twins' names in the same loud, worried voice he'd been using inside the house. He banged the side gate open and walked into the backyard. Jake started after him, feeling foolish. Of course. It was simple, after all, and there had been no reason to get so worried. They were in the backyard.

He followed his father, squinting to see into the increasing darkness, waiting for the wonderful sound of a giggle. He would never be mean to his sisters again, he promised himself and the universe. He would never yell at them or order them out of his room again. He would never wish they had never been born, or hope that they would get sick and have to stay in bed for a day or two to give him a break. He would be nice to them, and play with them more, and . . .

"Jake!" His father's voice cut into his thoughts. "Where are you?"

"Here!" Jake stopped in his tracks and realized that the backyard was silent. It was as unnaturally quiet as the house and the front yard. The twins were not here. Jake shivered. It was almost dark now, and it was getting chilly. He watched his father come closer, then turned to walk beside him as they headed back to the front yard. His father didn't say anything until they were back inside the house.

"I guess I should call the police."

Jake nodded. What else could they do?

Jake's father paced across the living room toward

the phone. After a few seconds, Jake heard him talking urgently. Jake stood and listened; it was hard to understand every word, but he could hear enough to know that his father was making a missing persons report to someone at the police station.

"Jake?" his father called, walking out of the living room, his hand over the receiver of the portable phone. "They're asking me what the twins were wearing when you saw them last."

Jake shook his head, trying to recall. He rarely noticed what the twins were wearing, unless Becca had put together one of her ridiculous orange plaid blouse and purple striped pants combinations. He wrinkled his forehead, straining to remember, to picture the girls as they had looked when he'd gotten home from school. Becca had had peanut butter or something on her face. He could remember that much clearly.

He shook his head, trying hard to think. Why couldn't he remember what they'd been wearing? He knew the answer: he had been too anxious to get upstairs to the bathroom so he could talk to the mirror man. He looked at his father. That wasn't something he wanted to tell his father about—especially now. His father was still staring at him, hoping for an answer. Jake shook his head again. "I don't know. I just can't remember."

Jake's father pulled in a deep breath. "Keep trying. If you think of it, come into the living room and tell me. It's okay, though. Your mother will

96

know. She can tell them, once I call her at work."
Jake watched his father turn and pace back toward
the living room. "I'll have to do that next," he said
over his shoulder. Jake felt sick. His father's voice
had dropped nearly to a whisper. He turned the
corner into the living room and Jake heard him
begin to talk into the receiver again. He estimated
how much the twins weighed and gave the police a
description of their size, and hair and eye color.

Jake stood very still, unable to do anything but
stare at the wall and listen to his father talk. He
felt awful, almost dizzy. How could this be happening? How could he have let it happen? He walked
toward the stairs. Was there anywhere they hadn't
looked? Maybe the twins had somehow gotten hurt
and couldn't answer when he called them. Jake
hesitated at the bottom of the stairs as an idea
hit him.

There was a tiny attic. Maybe the twins had
found the little door in their parents' room and had
gone through it. Jake started up the stairs, knowing it was unlikely, but feeling hope beating in his
heart anyway. He called the twins from the door of
his parents' room and got no answer. And even
though he knew it was useless, he slid the
nightstand away from the wall and swung open the
little door that led into the attic. He got down on
his knees and looked in. It was entirely dark.

"Becca? Tracy?" Jake peered into the darkness,
then reached back and opened the nightstand

drawer. His father's flashlight always had fresh batteries in it. Jake switched it on and shined it into the little attic space.

His mother's trunk was against one wall, as it always was. His father's tennis rackets and golf clubs were against the opposite wall. In between, the Christmas ornament boxes and an old radio were stacked. That was it. Jake stood up and closed the door.

"Good thought," his father said, from the doorway behind him.

Startled, Jake turned around. His father had the portable phone in his hand, holding it loosely.

His father ran a hand through his hair. "I still haven't called your mother. I'm about to."

Jake closed the door to the little storage attic and slid the nightstand back in front of it. Where could they be? He slammed the flashlight against his palm.

"Getting upset at yourself won't help," his father was saying. "The only thing we can do now is look and hope and pray that they're all right." Jake nodded. His father was right, but he hated to hear it, hated to admit it. His sisters were missing. Maybe they were hurt. Anything could have happened in the amount of time that had gone by since he'd checked on them. Jake rolled the silvery flashlight over in his hand, staring at it, thinking.

An all too familiar image came to life on the silver flashlight, distorted by its curve and the bright ridges molded into the metal. Jake blinked. The mirror man was smiling at him. And it was an awful, evil smile. Jake shivered, suddenly cold, his thoughts jolted into silence. The mirror man disappeared.

10

"I'm going to have to call your mother," Jake's father said quietly. Jake nodded, barely hearing him. His father turned and went back out into the hall. Jake followed, but walked more slowly. Did the mirror man have anything to do with Tracy and Becca being gone? By the time Jake got to the head of the stairs, his father was already at the bottom. Jake heard the little beeps that meant his father was dialing the restaurant.

Jake closed his eyes and swayed on his feet, wishing he'd been more responsible. He hadn't checked on the twins because they'd been quiet. Which was weird. He should have gotten suspicious. And their room was so neat, so perfectly clean. That was incredibly unusual, too, even if his mother had cleaned it right before she'd left. Maybe the twins had sneaked past his room right after he'd gone into it—maybe they hadn't played for more than a few minutes in their room after his mother had left. Nothing else would really explain it.

Jake imagined the way the twins' room usually looked, like a hurricane had hit a toy store. He even imagined their peanut butter–smeared faces and their squealing voices. He missed them, and he felt awful. All he wanted in the whole world was to go upstairs and have them jump out into the hallway and shriek and scream and want to play Sharks.

Jake heard an odd bumping noise, and he opened his eyes, looking down the hall toward the twins' room. His heart slamming against his ribs, he turned and ran down the hall. As he flipped on the lights, he found himself staring into the reflection that sprang to life on the night-darkened glass of the twins' window. The mirror man was leaning toward him, smiling and winking. "They certainly have been quiet, haven't they? Are you sure you—"

Jake reached out and jerked the window shade over the mirror man's reflection. The instant he did, Becca grabbed him from behind, tackling his legs and giggling madly. "Come on, Jake. We want to play Sharks. Can we? Will you play with us?"

Jake turned around and scooped her up as Tracy danced in a circle around them. *"Dad!"* Jake screamed out. "Dad, I found them!" Jake heard his father pounding up the stairs.

"Tracy! Becca!" his father cried out from the doorway, relief in his voice. "Thank God you're safe."

He came to kneel beside Jake and they each hugged one of the twins.

Suddenly Jake's father stood up, lifting Tracy with him. "I have to call your mother. I don't want her to worry a second more than she has to. I can't understand how this happened," he added, letting Tracy wriggle back to the floor. He was turning to dial the phone.

Jake was incredibly happy and relieved. But underneath those feelings was the strange and frightening realization that he had somehow been the cause of the twins' disappearance.

"Dad, I—" he began, but his father only shook his head, punching in the numbers of the restaurant on the portable phone. "They're fine, and that's what counts. I'll tell your mother, then we'll try to sort out how this happened. I want to catch her before she leaves. As upset as she was, she could have a wreck trying to get here fast."

Jake nodded and hugged his giggling sisters. They were so noisy that his father walked back out into the hall to make the phone call.

Jake glanced at the window shade. What had the mirror man asked him? If he was sure he wanted something. But what? It made Jake feel sick to think about the mirror man being so close to his sisters.

"Where were you two?" Jake asked Becca. She looked at him like he'd said something silly. He repeated the question.

"Here," Becca said. She patted the floor. "Where were you?"

"In my room," Jake told her. He waited a few seconds, then asked Tracy the same question.

"Mama told us to stay in our room and be quiet and be nice and not to bug you too much if we could help it." Tracy recited the whole list with one finger shaking back and forth—a gesture his mother used when she lectured the twins.

Jake shook his head and sighed, looking at the window shade again. Suddenly, he remembered imagining the twins gone, their room clean and quiet and *empty*.

When Jake's mother got home, they all sat in the living room for a while, talking about what had happened. That is, Jake sat and listened while his parents talked. Once or twice he opened his mouth, willing himself to tell them about the mirror man, to explain what he was beginning to believe about the power the mirror man had talked about. But he couldn't. How could he explain anything about the mirror man to his parents?

Jake watched his mother dab at her eyes with a tissue. She had cried a little, talking about how scared she'd been after Jake's father's first phone call. They both asked the twins where they had been and got the same kind of answers Jake had gotten.

Jake's mother sighed. "Maybe this'll be one of those crazy things that we'll never have an explanation for."

Jake's father nodded. "It sure makes no sense to me. Jake says he'd been looking for them for a few minutes before I came. And the two of us went all over this house."

"Were you two hiding?" Jake's mother asked the girls. Becca shook her head. Tracy ignored the question. It was about the twentieth time someone had asked it.

Jake's father stood up. "It's time for bed, ladies." He let the twins kiss their mother and Jake goodnight. Then he scooped them up and went slowly up the stairs, one twin perched on each hip. Jake was left alone with his mother.

"Are you all right?" she asked once the twins and his father had gone.

"I guess so," Jake said quietly. "I'm tired, I think. This is all pretty strange, Mom." He wanted to say more to her, but he just couldn't. He stood up and went upstairs. Once he was alone inside his room, he got undressed and went to bed. But of course he couldn't sleep.

Lying in the dark, Jake kept running through everything that had happened. He had talked to the mirror man, then he had gone into his room. The twins had disappeared. Jake turned over, then flopped onto his back again. It was dark, but he imagined that he could feel the presence of the mirror man.

Jake sat up in bed and swung his feet to the floor. He flipped on the light and looked into glass that covered his African poster. The outline was faint, but the mirror man was there. The instant Jake focused on his odd silhouette, he spoke.

104

"Hey, Jake, that was a good one. With your sisters. You shouldn't have brought them back so soon, though. All that noise this evening—"

Jake shook his head angrily. "What are you talking about?"

The mirror man grinned, the ghostly outlines of his teeth showing in the glass. "You know what I am talking about. The power. That perfect, empty room. So quiet, so peaceful."

Jake stared, stunned. He had no idea what to ask. He was afraid of the questions—and even more afraid of the answers. His heart was beating fast and his palms were sweaty. "I didn't mean to make them disappear," he blurted. His voice sounded like a little kid's, whiny and frightened.

The mirror man only laughed. "Don't be foolish, Jake," he said slowly. "That's *exactly* what you meant to do. You wished for it before. The difference is that now, you have the power." His image was fainter now, fading.

"Wait," Jake demanded. "I don't want any power. I—"

"That's not what you said this afternoon," the mirror man reminded him.

"I was just mad at Rob Phillips—"

"And your sisters, and your mother. Angry, angry Jake." The mirror man grinned again. His image got a little brighter, then softened and faded into nothingness. Jake stared into the empty glass.

The next day at school, Jake tried hard to just sit in his seat and stay out of everyone's way. He didn't feel like being there. In fact, he didn't feel like being anywhere that he could think of. Maybe Africa, if he could just watch wildebeests and gazelles and lions and didn't have to talk to anyone. There wouldn't be any mirrors out on the African plains, Jake thought. Or hubcaps or poster glass. Maybe that was the answer. He could run away—before he hurt his sisters or his parents or someone else by imagining terrible things.

"Psst."

Jake didn't turn his head. Rob had been trying all day to get his attention, but every time their eyes met, Jake made a point of looking away instantly. In fact, he had kept his eyes down most of the day, unless he was getting paper out of his notebook. Then he looked up at the ceiling. He was determined not to see the mirror man again—ever.

The bell rang and Jake jumped a little. He hadn't been watching the clock.

"Recess," Mrs. Richards announced. "Go out quietly, please, and stay in line until you're outside."

The classroom exploded into shuffling and banging as kids put their work inside their desks and got up to leave. The line formed quickly and Mrs. Richards opened the door. Jake waited until he saw Rob get in line, then he went forward. He considered staying inside to avoid Rob altogether, but then he decided against it.

"Want to play some football?" Don Blair was looking at him, smiling.

Jake shook his head. "Thanks. But I'm not very good."

"If you'd play more, you'd get better."

Jake looked at Don, grateful that he was a friendly person and that somehow he didn't seem as afraid to attract Rob's attention as everyone else was. But as much as Jake appreciated Don's invitation, he didn't want to play football right now. "Not today," he said to Don. "Thanks for asking, though. Maybe tomorrow."

Don nodded and headed for the ball box. Jake heard him lining up a few other boys to practice passing. For a few seconds, Jake stared at them. It would be very nice to be able to play football with two or three friends at recess. It would be very nice not to have to think about a bully like Rob all the time. Or the mirror man.

Jake took a deep breath. More than anything, he needed to get outside, to get away from everyone for a while. He didn't want to be on the playground, though. It would be crowded, and that was where Rob would be. Jake waited for the classroom to clear out a little. He saw Rob moving toward the ball box, too. Good. Maybe he'd be shooting baskets today.

Jake glanced around the room. Maybe he could go to the library. If he took the shortcut between the buildings, he'd be able to stay away from the basketball courts. That was where Rob would probably be. And he could stay out of the crowd almost completely. Jake waited until he saw Rob leave, then counted to fifty before he went out. Rob would probably assume he was going to stay in—he'd been staying in most of the time for quite a while now.

Outside the sun was shining. Jake blinked at the sky. The way he felt, he would have preferred a cloudy day. Besides, the sun made everything too shiny. He turned to walk along the side of the building. A few kids spent recess on the library steps, talking and reading. They were mostly the really studious kids, and some of the girls who would rather chat than play sports. Rob wouldn't look for him there. Jake walked faster.

The shortcut was a long quiet strip of lawn between the two buildings where almost no one ever went—Jake often used it to beat Rob back to the classroom on library day. If he could just get around the first corner, Rob would never know where he'd gone. Jake hurried, almost running. As he came out onto the deserted stretch of lawn, he exhaled. Perfect. Now he could—

"Hey! Jerk!"

Jake kept going, hoping he had not recognized the voice, or that for some unknown reason, Rob was picking on someone else for a change.

"Hey, jerk! I'm talking to you!"

Jake sighed. It was Rob, all right. What a great idea it had been to take the shortcut between the gym and the cafeteria. There was no one around.

"Hey!"

Jake refused to turn. He kept walking. He heard footsteps behind him coming up fast, then Rob's voice again. "Hey. My uncle is a cop. He asked me if I knew your family."

Jake faltered, then kept walking.

"I guess your dad wasted everyone's time the other night. All because you lost track of your sisters."

Unable to stop himself, Jake spun around. "Just leave me alone, Rob."

Rob sneered. "My uncle heard all about it from the guy who took the phone call from your dad. You found them in their room? How stupid are you, Jake? Why didn't you look there before you called the police? Where else would they be?"

"Just shut up," Jake interrupted Rob. "Just close your mouth. You have no idea what happened—"

"Are you calling my uncle a liar?" Rob demanded. "They took a whole missing persons report from your father. They would have typed it up and put it into the computer. Then, your dad calls back and says that gee, uh, you found your sisters in their room." Rob laughed again, an ugly, harsh sound that made Jake grit his teeth.

Jake tried to walk away, but Rob grabbed at his sleeve and turned him back around. Jake felt his cheeks flushing with anger. Rob pushed at his shoulder, knocking him off balance. "Did you get that black eye from walking into a wall somewhere? You're just about the dumbest kid in the world, you know that? What a jerk."

Jake stared at Rob, feeling his pulse in his temples. He ground his teeth together. "*You're* the jerk," he hissed at Rob.

Rob raised a hand fast, as though he were about to punch Jake. Jake flinched and Rob laughed again, moving around him. Jake kept turning to face him, so angry that he wasn't sure he could speak. He was afraid he would just sputter and stutter and give Rob something else to make fun of.

As they faced off, Jake glared at Rob, imagining his old favorite fantasy of Rob melting like gelatin, like the witch in *The Wizard of Oz*. He imagined it with all the fury that was inside him. He could just *see* it, in his mind—he could see every detail, especially the look of fear on Rob's usually mean face.

For a long moment, they just stared at each other. Jake began to hope that Rob would lose interest and leave him alone. Maybe he could see how much Jake hated him, how furious he was for all the mean things Rob had ever done.

Suddenly, Rob's eyes went wide with fear and Jake saw steam rising from his hair. Jake's fury dissolved into panic. He had been so angry, so furious at Rob for shoving him around and insulting him, that he had completely forgotten about the power. And what he'd suspected was true. If he imagined something vividly enough, it happened. Rob was melting.

Jake took a step back and watched, horrified, as Rob's feet dissolved. He staggered, gasping, a dark, sticky-looking puddle growing around his ankles. "Help me," Rob whispered. His face was pale, his eyes full of shock and terror. "Help me. Get someone. *Do something.*"

Panicked, his breath coming fast, Jake spun around. No one was nearby. Unless someone was watching through the small windows on this side of the cafeteria kitchen, no one would see. Unless he ran for help, no one would know what was happening. Jake took another step back. What could he do? He had to get someone. He turned away from Rob, half dizzy with disbelief. How could any of this be happening?

"Who will you get? And how could they help?"

It was the mirror man's voice, and Jake whirled

around. The mirror man was reflected in the puddle at Rob's feet. "Help," Jake stammered. "Please. Help me. I didn't really mean for this to happen. I—"

"You didn't?" the mirror man asked mildly. "You certainly seemed detailed and sure about it. Much clearer than you were about the twins. I had to help with that one."

Jake shook his head. Rob was clawing at his knees now, sinking into the sidewalk puddle. His mouth was open, and a constant stream of words poured out. He wasn't making very much sense now. It was horrible, more horrible than Jake had ever imagined it could be. His heart was hammering against his ribs. He had to do something. If he didn't, Rob was going to die. And what would happen the next time Jake got angry at his sisters? Or his parents? Or just about anyone? Without meaning to, he imagined it for a second.

The mirror man laughed. "That's it, Jake. The power can do all that and more. No one will ever dare pick on you or get in your way again."

Jake flinched at the sound of the mirror man's voice. Rob was flailing his arms back and forth now. The mirror man's face stretched, then rippled as Rob's fingers swept through the puddle of goo.

"Help me," Rob stammered. "I won't ever bother you again. I won't follow you home anymore. I'll never put anything in your desk or on your porch.

112

And I'll never mess with your homework . . . Jake, please. Help me."

Jake shook his head, feeling helpless. At least with the twins, everything had turned out all right. Jake felt understanding seeping into him. He had imagined the twins coming back. Maybe he could fix this, too. The twins hadn't been hurt or melting, though. If whatever he could imagine would come true, then all he had to do was imagine that Rob was fine. The mirror man laughed again and Jake's thoughts scattered. "Nothing is funny!" he screamed. "Make this stop." He gestured at Rob.

The mirror man shook his head. "I can't."

Jake stared at the mirror man. His face was clear now, as if the puddle were chrome silver instead of dark, sticky ooze. Jake felt his cheeks heating up again; he was more angry than he'd ever thought he could get. And his anger wasn't directed at Rob, for once. Or his sisters, or anyone else. The target of Jake's rage was the mirror man, smiling his weird smile. Careful not to let himself think about it too long or too hard, Jake suddenly stared down at the mirror man.

"No!" the mirror man shouted. "Rob's the one, not me."

Jake didn't allow himself to look away. He centered his anger and his thoughts and aimed them at the distorted face in the horrible puddle on the sidewalk. With every slamming beat of his pulse, he concentrated harder.

113

As Rob sank lower, his mouth gaping, Jake imagined him standing up, whole and safe again, while the mirror man melted into nothingness, evaporating like mist in a wind. Jake switched the two images back and forth in his mind, adding details, making them as clear and perfect as he could. He imagined Rob smiling, whole, the way he'd always been. And he imagined the mirror man disappearing forever: every mirror, every shining surface, reflecting only what it should.

Jake heard muted voices, but he kept his fury and his attention focused. He remembered all the days he'd had to avoid looking at anything shiny, all the times he'd been scared and too afraid to tell anyone what was happening to him.

After a few seconds, the puddle began shrinking and Rob began growing taller. With every ounce of energy he had, Jake kept his concentration burning, turned up high. He imagined Rob walking away and the mirror man vaporizing into a mist that would blow away on the wind, scattered into molecules. He imagined the rest of his life without a mirror man to make it miserable.

"No!" the mirror man shrieked, his face swirling in the rapidly shrinking puddle. A few moments later, there was a little puff of mist. A sudden breeze scattered the vapor mist around Rob's legs as he stood, his mouth open, staring at Jake.

"I'm s-sorry for what I said about your sisters," he managed. "I'm sorry about everything. Just please don't ever do anything like that . . ." He stopped, breathing hard, staring at Jake.

Jake was nearly doubled over, exhausted, his breath ragged and uneven. He had never been so tired in his whole life. Or so happy. He smiled at Rob, feeling giddy. "Just leave me alone, Rob. That's all I want. Leave everybody alone. Stop picking on people."

Rob nodded, so hard and fast that he looked silly. "I will. I sure will. I absolutely will. And I'm sorry. For everything." Rob looked like he was going to say something else, but then he closed his mouth. Jake watched him pat himself up and down, as though he was checking to make sure his body was where it should be. Then he turned and walked away, very slowly at first, as though he was testing his legs with every step. He looked back at Jake twice, then just kept going.

Jake looked down at the sidewalk. There was a faint pattern in the cement, as though something had stained it. If you looked at it just right, it almost looked like a face—nearly human, but with something a little strange about it. Jake scuffed his shoe across it. Then he walked away, going in the same direction Rob had gone.

Jake felt weak, as though it had taken all his strength to keep Rob from melting. But he also felt good. He wobbled his way to the library steps and sat down. It was a sunny day. He squinted up at

115

the sky, then at the kids around him. It was a beautiful day.

As he sat, his breath evening out, Jake found himself smiling. It was a wonderful day. He was almost looking forward to going home after school and playing with his sisters for a while. Then he was going to go across the street and see if Don Blair wanted to play football. Maybe if he practiced more, he'd get better at it. One thing he knew for sure: he was never going to get as angry at the twins again.

Jake was still sitting on the steps when Rob wobbled by. He looked up at Jake and blinked. Jake knew he was wondering if what had happened could possibly be real. Jake knew the feeling well. Rob went past, glancing back once or twice, but not stopping. Maybe in a few days he'd tell Rob about the mirror man. Rob was the one person in the whole world who just might believe him. Jake grinned. Maybe he'd ask Rob if he thought the mirror man had somehow grown out of how angry he was at everything . . . was that possible? If it was, he was gone for good. Jake was never going to let anything bother him enough to make it happen again.

Jake looked around, staring intently at the shiny bumpers of cars in the parking lot, at the library windows. Everything looked wonderfully, perfectly normal. Reflections were just reflections again. The girl sitting just ahead of Jake on the steps pulled a little mirror out of her jeans pocket and began to comb her hair.

"Can I see that for a second?" Jake asked.

She turned and handed him the mirror, then turned back to say something to one of her friends. Jake held the mirror close, his heart racing a little, even though he knew what he would see: a boy with a fading black eye and a big grin. There was no doubt left in his mind now. He had created the mirror man without meaning to—but he had destroyed him with every ounce of his own determination and will. It was over. The mirror man was gone for good.

Midnight came to Marville, Massachusetts. November 21 had finally arrived.

At that exact moment, in a dimly lit room hidden underneath one of Marville's more respectable businesses, something very weird was about to happen.

A middle-aged man (who was usually in bed long before midnight) found himself sitting on the cold hard floor staring down at an old weather-beaten book. Then, powered by forces he could not see, he started singing,

> *"Happy birthday to you.*
> *Happy birthday to you.*
> *Happy birthday, Mike Jacobs.*
> *Happy birthday to you."*

Mike Jacobs, now officially thirteen years old, was sleeping safe and sound in his bed on the other side of town. He's lucky he wasn't there to witness the serenade . . . for three reasons.

Reason #1: The guy performing the tune wasn't a very good singer. You might say he stunk. Not only that, but for some strange reason he couldn't finish a line of the song without breaking into a laugh. Then he'd stop, look around, wonder what in the world was happening to him, and pick up where he'd left off. So it actually sounded more like this:

"Happy birthday to you-ou-ou-ou . . . Hee . . . Hee hee . . . Hmmph hmmph haa haa . . . HAH HAH HAH HAAAH HEEEEE HEEEEEE HAAAH HOOOOW HARRRRRRRRRRRRRR!" Stop. Look around dimly lit room with really confused look on face. Start again.

Reason #2: Although he was a normal-looking guy, the singer kept twisting his face into a freak-ish sneer. And if you ventured close enough, you would have sworn that his tongue was a dull shade of green.

Reason #3: The singer was sharpening a very long knife.

At that same moment in another part of town, someone else was thinking of Mike Jacobs. He was an old man. Very old. So old, in fact, that if you met him you would have thought that he was dead

119

and just hadn't realized it yet. He might have agreed with you, but he was too busy reading his books.

They were piled up on the desk all around him. There were big ones and little ones, old ones and new ones. And if you had the guts to get really close, you might even have noticed the titles on a few of them: *The Illustrated Encyclopedia of Demons, Supernatural Occurrences in New England,* and *A History of Evil.*

The old man had spent most of the past six months of his life doing the same thing every day. He'd sleep all day and get up just as the sun was setting. He didn't bother brushing his teeth or hair. Why should he? He rarely set foot outside his door and nobody *ever* came to visit.

He'd light a candle and sit at the desk. Then he'd read through the books as he stroked his very long and very gray beard. But he never found what he was looking for. So the only thing he managed to scribble on his note pad was a name. The same name that he had written over and over and over again, until the entire pad was filled with the same name: *Mike Jacobs.*

But tonight was different. When midnight came, the old man knew that the time was here. November 21 was Mike Jacobs's thirteenth birthday, and that could mean only one thing: An ancient evil was about to be unleashed on Marville. And he was powerless to do anything about it.

But the midnight birthday party of Mike Jacobs was not over yet. Not quite, that is. You see, there was one more person eagerly awaiting the arrival of November 21.

Imprisoned in a world of nothingness, he—*it*—somehow knew that today he would finally get his chance to roam through the streets of Marville once again. Then it would only be a matter of time before he got what he had dreamed about for centuries—revenge.

"Revenge . . ." he growled to himself. "Revenge on every living relative of the man who sent me to this place of nothingness!"

For the past four hundred years he'd been held captive in the place of endless night. But that time was at an end.

For on November 21, Mike Jacobs was turning thirteen. And he was getting a birthday gift he would never forget.

ABOUT THE AUTHOR

Novelist M.T. COFFIN, whose "Spinetinglers" novels have sold more than one million copies, began his career writing obituaries as a freelancer for his local newspaper, *The Nightly Caller*. This was in addition to his full-time job in the Dead Letter Department of the post office. While he thoroughly enjoyed writing about the dead, M.T. Coffin abandoned that work to begin his first novel when a series of nightmares so amused and delighted him that he felt he must write them down to share with his friends and family. He wrote thirteen "Spinetinglers" before his wife, Berry A. Coffin, convinced him that the stories were interesting and exciting enough to share with others and helped him to submit his manuscripts to Avon Books for possible publication. The books were accepted immediately and the "Spinetinglers" series was born when the first novel, *The Substitute Creature,* was published in March 1995.

Gwen Montgomery, of the Young Readers Department at Avon Books, is delighted to be publishing M.T. Coffin and says, "My spine tingled on the very first page and I knew right then that M.T. Coffin's books would keep readers dying for more."

M.T. Coffin was born on October 31 in Death Valley, California. The year is uncertain since, for some mysterious reason, all records of his birth except the date have disappeared, and no records of any family members have ever been discovered. Raised as an orphan, M.T. Coffin attended Death Valley High School. After graduation, he attended DeKay University where he studied literature. It was there that he was introduced to the works of authors who were to be among his lifelong favorites, including Bram Stoker, Mary Shelley, H.G. Wells, Jules Verne, Mark Twain, and Edgar Allan Poe. It was also there that he met Berry during a blood drive on campus. Berry received a Bachelor of Arts degree in elementary education from DeKay and today is a substitute teacher and bee keeper.

Now, M.T. Coffin is writing full-time and has just completed *Boogey's Back for Blood.* Works in progress include *Lights, Camera, Die!, Camp Crocodile,* and *Gimme Back My Brain.* He is currently traveling to research upcoming novels and has most recently visited Transylvania in Romania and Murderers Creek, Oregon. Other "Spinetinglers" by M.T. Coffin include *Billy Baker's Dog Won't Stay Buried, My Teacher's a Bug, Where Have All the Parents Gone?, Check It Out—and Die!, Simon Says, "Croak!,"* and *Snow Day.*

M.T. Coffin lives in Tombstone, Arizona, with

Berry and their two children, Phillip A. Coffin and Carrie A. Coffin, and their dog, Bones. He enjoys many hobbies, including reading, collecting books, taxidermy, playing the pipe organ, and bug collecting, an activity the entire family enjoys. The Coffins split their time between Arizona and their summer vacation home in Slaughter Beach, Delaware.

When asked about "Spinetinglers" and his many readers, M.T. Coffin responds, "I get goosebumps every time I think about how exciting it is to be able to tell stories all the time, and to reach so many people. I plan to keep writing forever."